The Cowboy and Hi Best Friend's Daughter

Kaci M. Rose

D1603621

Five Little Roses Publishing

Copyright

Book Cover By: **Sarah Kil Creative Studio**

Editing By: Debbe @ **On The Page, Author and PA Services**

To Liz and Marissa,

You two have gotten me through all the ups and downs in life so I dedicate this series to you.

I hope you find some laughter, a few characters like you, and a little revenge to some unfinished business.

Thank you for being my friend even when we are states apart.

Blurb

Jenna

Everyone thinks I'm the aimless lost little girl.

But the truth is I'm falling for my dad's best friend.

He's everything I never thought I wanted.

I spend my days writing my novel or working in the diner – dreaming of a different life.

With Josh, my dreams aren't about leaving Walker Lake anymore.

Every moment I'm near him, I crave his touch.

Small-town gossip and the man I shouldn't want could ruin my life forever.

Josh

I know better than to want Jenna.

My best friend would lose his mind if he knew how much I dreamed about a life with his daughter.

When she's with me, I feel at ease.

She's beautiful and kind.

Watching her on my ranch makes me think we might have a chance.

But falling for Jenna could mean losing everything else.

Contents

Get Free Books!

Would you like some free cowboy books?

If you join Kaci M. Rose's Newsletter you get books and bonus epilogues free!

Join Kaci M. Rose's newsletter and get your free books!

https://www.kacirose.com/KMR-Newsletter

Now on to the story!

Chapter 1
JOSH

"You're going to join us for the 4th of July festivities downtown, right, Josh?" my best friend Evan asks.

I'm having dinner at his house like I do every week. Every Sunday is family dinner with his four kids and his wife, and they are gracious enough to include me since I am unmarried and have no children.

"Of course. I really enjoyed it last year. There's just something about a small-town July 4th celebration that beats out any of the big town ones we've celebrated. Plus, the boys put on a hell of a show with sparklers last year. I think we need a repeat," I say. Though at the same time, I'm trying to pull my head out of the clouds and back into the conversation.

"I couldn't agree more," Evan says with a grin.

"Hell yeah. That was so much fun," Finn says. He's the middle of the three boys and a daredevil. He rides in the rodeo to earn money for the ranch the boys plan on buying but also for the thrill of it. I'm sure the attention from the girls doesn't hurt, though it has earned him a playboy reputation.

"Don't encourage them! They almost burned the deck down last year!" Evans's wife says.

"Mom, we weren't even close to burning it down. Plus, we are more experienced this year." Zach, the youngest brother, joins the conversation.

Janet gives the boys the 'I'm your mother, don't start with me look,' and I can't help the chuckle that escapes. Though when Jenna looks up at me from across the table, she's got a small smile on her face. She was nothing but my best friend's little girl, running around in pigtails and starting her first day of school. Then, somewhere after her sixteenth birthday, she had a pool party and walked out in this lacy black bikini, and suddenly, she was no longer a little girl in my eyes.

After that, I stopped coming around claiming some big projects at work, and even moved away for a few years.

When their youngest child, Jenna, turned eighteen, they bought their place out here in the small town of Walker Lake, Texas. Once they moved here, I started to come for visits figuring enough time had passed. But the first time that I saw Jenna after all those years, I was about knocked off my feet.

I tried to keep my distance, but a few years ago, a ranch came up for sale in town, and Jenna was gushing over how much she loved the house on it and all the old details. Before I knew it, I was the proud owner of that ranch, and I moved here to Walker Lake. She was twenty-one.

Now, it's been two years of Sunday dinners, and I've managed to keep my distance. Not that she's really made it easy. Though I'm guessing she doesn't know what she does to me because there's no way she's interested in her father's best friend, who's fifteen years older than her.

"He'll take me on the rides again this year, won't you, Josh?" Jenna asks.

It's such an innocent question for everyone else at the table, but what she's asking is if I'll be going on the rides that will push us together, and many of them end up with her almost in my lap. But the way she laughs and smiles, there's no way I would tell her no.

"Of course, that is as long as no one else here wants to go with you," I say.

Since Jenna's brothers are currently looking to buy a ranch together to run, I'm sure they'll be more interested in networking with other ranchers. There's always a big animal show on the 4th of July, so that's where they will be spending their time.

Jenna's parents like to walk around and look at all the booths and crafts and spend their time tasting food. They have no interest in the rides.

"We wouldn't dare break tradition this year. Besides, I heard the diner has a food booth this year, and they're trying out some new recipes to see what the town likes so they can add it to their menu. We can't miss that," Jenna's mom, Janet, says, reaching out to take Evan's hand in hers.

They've been sweethearts since middle school, and to see them still so head over heels in love gives me hope that maybe someday, I can still have that. But to find it, I have to get Jenna out of my system.

"Yes, Austin has been trying some new recipes. I even heard they will start offering more homemade pies. Her sister Natalie has been experimenting with some new recipes," Asher says.

I haven't known that boy to turn down anything sweet in my life.

As the conversation continues, my mind keeps wandering back to Jenna. She's sitting across the table from me, wearing a simple sundress that's hugging her curves in all the right places. Even though I try to divert my gaze, my eyes keep returning to her. She's grown into such a beautiful woman, and it's hard for me not to let my mind wander to what it would be like to have her in my arms. But I can't let myself go there. She's too young for me, and besides, she is my best friend's daughter.

"I almost forgot. I got a lead on a ranch. It needs a lot of work, from what I'm told. Though it hasn't been worked in a few years, and it's further out of town than we were looking at, but I'm going to try to set up a meeting to take a look," Asher says.

He's always been more of the take-control one. Finn and Zach are working just as hard to earn money for the ranch, but Asher has been the lead on looking. Now that they are close to buying, they have an idea of what is out there.

"Let us know, and I'm happy to go with you and take a look," Evan says.

"Me too. A woman's touch on the house you will be living in, even for a short time, is always needed!" Janet says.

"Of course, we want your opinions," Finn says.

I know they have already looked at one ranch, but it was smaller than they wanted. Also, Evan caught quite a few things they had missed that would make it impossible for them to get up and go with in a year like they had planned. Things like how the fence had to be replaced, and half the pastures were unusable as they hadn't been taken care of properly. The deciding factor for them not buying the property was that alfalfa had started to grow in a few of the fields, which can be toxic to cattle.

It's also a pain in the ass to get rid of and would prevent them from working the ranch for a good year. So, they reluctantly passed on that ranch. I know it was hard for them because ranches in this area don't go up for sale often, especially not at the lower price point they are looking at.

After dinner, Evan and I go for a walk along the edge of the lake. They bought a beautiful house right on the lake when they moved here, and one of our favorite things to do is talk and enjoy the beauty.

I'm drawn to the way the moonlight bounces off the water and the way the cool breeze feels on my skin. When I glance over at Evan, he appears content and relaxed. He's found his happiness, and I immediately squash my envy at his happiness. I want that, too.

"Are you okay, Josh?" Evan asks, breaking me out of my thoughts.

Shaking my head, I force a smile.

"Yeah, just a lot going on. I have a new horse being delivered tomorrow and was making sure I have everything in order." It's not a complete lie. I do have a horse being delivered. Only it is just the furthest thing from my mind. As always, Jenna was front and center. What would she look like in the moonlight? What would it be like to be walking with her along the lake instead of Evan?

Pushing those thoughts aside, I focus on my friend. He deserves my full attention.

"Janet and I have a favor to ask of you, and we know it's a big one," Evan says after we are away from the house.

"What's that?" I ask since he now has my attention, and my curiosity spiked.

"While you are talking to Jenna and going on the rides, will you see if you can encourage her to submit her books to publishers? We know she is done or almost finished with it. We've heard her talking about it with her friends. Why she seems so hesitant to submit it, we're not aren't sure why."

Ever since she graduated from college, Jenna has been writing a book. It's been her dream, and her parents have supported it, which is why she's been living with them while she learns and writes. At the same time, she's been working at the diner to meet people and get ideas on character building. At least, that's what she tells us.

Personally, I think she took the job because she wanted to get out of the house and earn some money herself. Not that she needs it. Evan was really good at what he did and investing in the stock market. They don't ever have to worry about money, and they've been taking care of Jenna.

I know they're really proud of their boys too, who are insistent on saving the money and buying the ranch without their parents' help. Of course, that means it's going to take them longer to get going and up on their feet.

"Yeah, I'll talk to her. My guess is there's something holding her back," I say.

I don't like the idea that fear could be stopping her from achieving something that she's been working so hard for. This is something she really wants, and I will do anything and move oceans to make it happen for her.

"I don't know if she's just scared to submit the book or if it's the fear of the unknown. But maybe she'll open up to you, as you two always seem to have a special bond," Evan says.

At his words, instantly guilt hits me. I was always Uncle Josh growing up, but as she hit those adult years, she stopped calling me Uncle Josh, and it became just Josh. Our relationship has definitely changed. What we discuss is much more adult, and I definitely don't see her as the little girl she used to be.

When we talk, the conversation flows better than any date I've ever been on in my life. Even though we have known each other for so long, there isn't ever a lack of things to discuss.

"I'll feel her out. It will come up anyway because we haven't talked in a while. I've been busy with the ranch, and we haven't seen each other much this summer." Though in reality, I've just been avoiding her.

It's easier to spend time with her when it's cold out, and she's all bundled up. However, on the chance of running into her in another bikini, I stay away in the summer. With the exception of events like the July 4th festival and Sunday night dinners where I make it a point that we aren't alone together.

"Well, I should head home and get ready for tomorrow," I say. In reality, if I go back inside, I'll be drawn to Jenna, and who knows where that could lead.

We say goodbye, and I leave. My best friend was none the wiser about the completely inappropriate thoughts I'd been having of his daughter all night.

Chapter 2
JENNA

I'm going to the July 4th festival from my friend Sky's house. She and her husband Dash are coming later to get a taste of some of the food offerings. We had breakfast together so we could catch up since it had been a few weeks. Summer is a busy time of year for any cowboy, and it's no different for their ranch. Any time we can fit it in, we get together. Today, it was brunch.

I'm halfway into town when my mom calls.

"Hey, Mom, what's up?" I expect her to tell me that she's going to be delayed since I'm supposed to be meeting her, Dad, and Josh there in about thirty minutes.

"Remember that ranch Asher was telling us about the other night at dinner?" Mom asks.

"Yeah, the one that's kind of run-down?"

"Yes, well, he finally got them to agree to a ranch tour, but only if we go now. So, your dad and I are going to meet them out there, and we won't be back until later this evening. We want you to still go to the July 4th festival with Josh so that he gets out of the house. You know he doesn't get out much, and your dad worries about him," Mom says.

"Well, I hope that it's what they're looking for, and I'll miss you guys. But there's no way I'm missing the festival. It's one of my favorites throughout the year."

"Okay sweetie, will you let Josh know what's going on? We're about to hit a dead zone, so I don't have time to call him."

"I'll let him know. Be safe, Mom, and I love you."

"We love you too, sweetheart," Mom says before the line goes dead.

A flock of butterflies takes flight in my stomach as I think about spending the whole day with Josh. Just me and him. We don't get much alone time together anymore as he seems to avoid being alone with me as if his life depends on it.

I have no idea what could be going on with him, but I know that I'll find out eventually.

Once I'm in town, I battle the traffic for a parking spot. Thankfully, Austin said I can park behind the diner. The diner itself is closed today. As I walk around the side of the building and into the chaos of the downtown square, I find Austin and Natalie with their both set up in front of the diner. They have enough food to feed our small army of hungry cowboys. This is also where I'm supposed to meet Josh.

"Hey girl!" Austin greets me as I approached her booth. "What's going on?"

"Well, my parents bailed on me, so it's just me and Josh today."

"Bummer," Natalie says.

"Not really. Josh is the one who will ride the rides with me."

We don't get to chat much longer because I see Josh walking up and move to meet him.

Simply watching Josh approach, I can feel my heart racing faster and my cheeks flushing red with excitement. It's been a while since we've hung out alone, and I'm looking forward to spending time with him.

He looks good, as always, in his tight jeans, cowboy hat, and boots. When our eyes meet, I can feel the butterflies dance in my stomach. After he gives me a small smile and a nod, he turns to Austin and Natalie to say hello.

He turns back to me, and I enjoy his eyes on me for a minute before he breaks the trance.

"Your mom and dad almost here?" he asks, looking behind me.

"No, Mom called on my way here to tell me that the boys got a tour of the ranch Asher was talking about at dinner. So, they are heading out there."

"Ahh, I should go home then, too. Lots to do," he says.

"Mom said that you would say that, and she told me to not let you hide away all day and to make sure that you stayed and enjoyed the festival. Don't get me in trouble with my mom because you ran home and hid." I try to apply a little guilt, but if it gets him to stay and spend the day with me, it's worth it.

He looks up over my head and seems to stare at something behind me, but I don't back down. When his eyes meet mine again, he smiles and nods his head.

"Alright, let's go get on some of the rides while everyone's getting lunch," he says.

When he says that, I have to stop myself from jumping for joy.

I want him to see me as a grown adult, an equal, so maybe he can realize I am more than just the kid he used to know. Maybe one day he can even see me as someone he would date because I've had a crush on him since I was about sixteen and started to like boys.

I was never interested in boys my own age. They all seemed so immature and awkward. Then I'd spend the weekend with Josh, and he was so calm and in control, so sure of himself. Though, I didn't really admit my feelings for him until he started to appear in all my late-night dreams. After that, I was done.

In college, I tried dating and even had a serious boyfriend. But when I knew I was moving back home, I ended it because I was more excited about seeing Josh than spending any amount of time with my boyfriend.

Bringing myself back to the present, I'm determined to enjoy every bit of this day with Josh and not waste any time.

We spend the next several hours on the rides. As we run from ride to ride, I can feel the adrenaline pumping through my veins. Every time we go on a new ride, I can't help but let out a scream of excitement. Josh seems to be enjoying himself, too, laughing and joking as we go up and down, around and around, at high speeds.

He shows just how well he knows me by picking all my favorite rides. We laugh and scream like little kids, lost in the thrill of the moment. It feels so good to let go and have fun with him like this.

"Okay, let's get some food in you before you get too cranky." He tells me after we finish up our second round of bumper cars.

I want to protest and ride some more, but he's right. I will get hangry if we wait much longer for me to eat.

Not even asking me what I want, he takes me right to the street taco booth and orders my favorites down to no tomatoes. Of course, he has to also get us a funnel cake.

"Come on, let's take our food and watch the kid's rodeo." He nods toward the arena.

Once again, he nails it. The kid's rodeo is one of my favorite parts of the festival. I love watching the little kids try their best to stay on the backs of the sheep and calves as they buck and thrash around. It has all the thrills of the rodeos Finn rides in, but a lot less danger and injuries.

We find a good spot near the fence and settle in, our plates of food balanced on our laps. As we watch the kids, I'm hyper aware of Josh's muscles rippling through his shirtsleeves as he laughs and claps along with the crowd. I've always found his strength and confidence incredibly attractive. But his powerful physique is a marvel of tight muscles that catches the eye. So there's no way I'm going to lose this opportunity to let my eyes wander over his body.

"Hey, you okay over there?" He asks, catching me watching him and snapping me out of my thoughts.

I quickly turn my gaze back to the rodeo, feeling a blush rise to my cheeks. "Yeah, I'm fine," I reply, trying to play it cool.

But Josh doesn't let it go. "Are you sure? You were staring pretty hard," he says, a playful glint in his eye.

I feel myself getting more flustered, but I can't deny the attraction I feel towards him any longer. "I'm sorry, I just can't help it. You're so... handsome," I blurt out, feeling a surge of bravery.

Josh's eyes widen, clearly surprised by my confession. But then he smiles, a slow, seductive grin that makes my heart race. "Is that so? You know, you're looking pretty damn good today, too."

His words catch me off guard, and heart starts to race. Is he flirting with me? Could it be possible that he feels the same way I do?

"Thanks, Josh," I say, trying to keep my voice steady.

Just then, the crowd erupts in cheers and clapping, pulling us from the moment, and we both focus back on the rodeo.

Things stay light as we watch the rest of the kids, and there isn't any awkwardness that you might expect.

"Want to walk some of the craft booths?" He asks after we finish up with the rodeo.

"Yeah, I ate way too much. I need to walk it off anyway," I joke.

We start walking around the square that is blocked off from traffic and lined with rows and rows of booths.

"So, how's your book coming along?" he asks. While I knew this question was coming, inwardly, I cringe. Josh had always been supportive of my dream to become a writer, but I haven't made much progress on my book in the past few months. After hitting a major writer's block on how to end the book and wrap it all up, I can't seem to shake it off.

"Uh, it's... coming along," I say hesitantly, not wanting to disappoint him.

But Josh can see right through my answer. "That doesn't sound too convincing," he says with a knowing look.

I sigh, knowing I can't keep hiding from the truth. "Honestly, I've hit a wall. I just can't seem to find a way to end the book and wrap it all up into a pretty bow that I'm happy with."

Josh nods understandingly, and I can see the gears turning in his head. "Well... what if you take a break from the book and focused on something else? Maybe a change of scenery or activity will help clear your mind," he suggests.

After considering his words for a moment, I nod in agreement. Maybe he's right. A change of pace could be just what I need to get my creative juices flowing again. Certainly sitting and staring at the screen every night isn't working.

"It can't hurt to try," I say as we walk into a booth filled with home decor items.

I pick up a few items for my room, and Josh is right there paying for them before I can even pull out my wallet.

"Thank you for these," I tell him.

He spoils me even more with some baked goods, a few books, and a necklace. As we complete our round at the booths, I'm noticing how much this feels like a date. There is such an ease as we walk, talk, laugh and joke. Things are so effortless between us.

I've always wondered what a date between us would be like, and I think it would be a lot like this. Just comfortable and fun enjoying spending time with each other. There wouldn't be any awkward first date because we already know each other so well.

As the sun gets ready to set, and we're walking back to the car, I say, "Thanks for hanging out with me today."

"No problem. I had a great time," Josh responds, his voice deep and smooth.

I turn to look at him, and our eyes meet again.

"Let's put your stuff in your car and go take a ride on the Ferris wheel and watch the sunset. You game?" he asks.

"That sounds great and yes," I say.

He walks with me, and I place the bags in the trunk of my car, and we head out to get in line at the Ferris wheel. Thankfully, there isn't much of a wait.

The town always sets the Ferris wheel up in the same place every year. It's so they can take advantage of the lake views. On your descent, you have the most beautiful views, the kind that would make a great postcard.

It's the style of Ferris wheel where only two people fit in a car. With Josh and me in the same car, there is no extra room. I'm pushed up to his side, so he places his arm on the back of the car behind me to give me extra room. Though I have to say, it does give it a romantic feel.

As we slowly rise above the ground, my heart beats faster and faster. It's not just because of the height, but because of the tension between Josh and me. Our bodies are so close together, and I feel his warmth seeping into me. When I turn my head to look at him, he's staring out across the lake with a small smile on his face. He looks so handsome in the golden glow of the sun setting. How can I possibly resist taking a minute to appreciate him? I let my eyes linger on his beautiful blue eyes, his strong jawline and those broad shoulders.

As we get to the top of the Ferris wheel and the sun begins its descent, my eyes are riveted on the breathtaking view. The orange and pink hues of the sunset reflect on the lake below, making it visually stunning.

"Wow." Josh says, breaking the silence.

I can feel his eyes on me. When I turn to face him, my heart skips a beat. He's looking at me with such intensity that I feel my cheeks flush.

"You're beautiful," he whispers like he's scared someone will hear us up here.

The butterflies in my stomach flutter and then take flight.

When the Ferris wheel stops with us at the top, I look at him and my heart beats faster than ever before. The look in his eyes is one I can't describe, but it leaves me breathless. He reaches his hand out and brushes a strand of hair out of my face before lightly tracing my jawline, his touch sending shivers down my spine.

"I've wanted to do this for so long," he says, leaning in slowly.

I know he's going to kiss me, and I can't wait to feel his lips on mine. I've waited so long for this kiss, so when the Ferris wheel jerks and starts moving, pulling us from the moment I want to scream. Josh sits back with a look of regret in his eyes. As the Ferris wheel starts going down, I'm awash with regret and disappointment. I wanted that kiss more than anything, but the moment has passed, and now we're back to being just friends. Or are we? I can't read Josh's expression, and it's driving me crazy. Does he regret almost kissing me? Or does he regret not kissing me?

When we step out of the car, the tension between us is thick. Even though I can feel his eyes on me, I can't bring myself to look at him just yet.

"Ready to go watch some fireworks?" he asks.

He's not trying to bolt. That's a good sign, right?

Chapter 3
JOSH

Holy shit, I almost kissed her. If the Ferris wheel hadn't started moving when it did, I would have kissed her no doubt about it. What I wouldn't give to know what her lips taste like, what it felt like to hold her in my arms, to cradle her close to me.

"I have a blanket in my truck. Let's grab it and then find a place to watch the fireworks," I say. With everything in me, I'm trying to keep things normal between us. The last thing I want to do is spook her and lose out on any more time together.

"Actually, if you are up for a short drive, I know a place where we can watch the fireworks away from the crowds," she says, surprising me.

"Alright, let's do it," I say.

Weaving in and out of the crowd that's all heading towards the lake, we go to my truck. While we walk, I can feel her gaze on me. It's like she's analyzing every move I make, trying to figure out what I'm thinking. It's no surprise that I really like her eyes on me.

When we get there, I open the truck door and help her inside, making sure she's buckled up before closing the door and getting in on my side. Starting the engine, I turn on the radio, scanning through the stations until I find one playing a soft rock song. It's the perfect background music for the drive.

Jenna gives me directions, taking us to the east side of the lake, and down a residential road. It's the same one that leads to her parents. Her parents' dock is a great place to view fireworks, but I'm not sure I want to be somewhere that Evan might find us.

"We going to your parents' place?" I ask wanting to mentally prepare myself.

"Nope. See that stone mailbox there? Pull into that driveway." She points to a house on my left.

Once I pull into the long driveway, a cabin comes into view. "Whose place is this?" I was not able to recall whose house it is.

"My friend Sarah, it's her husband's family cabin. They live in Rock Springs and do July 4th down there. They told me I can come here and use the patio and the deck any time I want."

We get out, and I grab the blanket from the truck for us to sit on. Then we walk around the side of the cabin. From the front it looks normal sized, but once you get to the side you realize it's really long and much bigger than you expected.

The deck is massive, and there are stone stairs leading down to the lake, with a large dock and patio swing at the end.

"They just added the patio swing the last time they were here. It's now my favorite spot to come and enjoy the lake. I will read out here or come to enjoy the sunset," she says as we go down to the dock.

As we make our way to the end of the dock, there's a sense of excitement building within me. I have Jenna all to myself. While this has been something I have been avoiding, right now I'm really looking forward to it.

Jenna settles on the swing, and I sit next to her, pulling the blanket over us. It might have been a hot July day, but the breeze that comes over the lake once the sun sets can give you a nice chill.

As the fireworks start on the other side of the lake, she snuggles up to my side, and I hesitantly wrap an arm around her.

The fireworks light up the night sky in a kaleidoscope of colors, reflecting off the calm surface of the lake. Jenna's head rests on my shoulder, and it feels right holding her in my arms, her body so warm and inviting. When she cuddles into me, not only is my heart racing, but I'm getting aroused as well. The fireworks continue to light up the sky, but my mind is focused solely on Jenna. It surprises me how intense and strong my feelings are for her.

While I knew I liked her, I guess I never let myself really go there and explore those feelings. Now it's like a damn broke and the feelings I had been keeping at bay rush over me.

The explosions in the sky seem to set off explosions in my heart. It's so easy to get lost in the moment with her. Like she can feel my eyes on her, she looks up at me and our eyes lock. There's something special in that gaze, a connection that feels as if it's been preordained. I brush a stray strand of hair from her face and lean in, finally giving in to the overwhelming urge to kiss her. Our lips meet, and then nothing else in the world exists. It's just Jenna and I, lost in the moment of our passionate kiss.

It feels like fireworks are going off in my mind, and my heart races as I feel her lips mold perfectly to mine.

Jenna responds eagerly, wrapping her arms around my neck as we deepen the kiss. It's like we have been waiting for this moment, both of us needing this connection. I cup the back of her head, holding her close to me, not letting my mind try to reason with my heart.

Laying her on her back on the deck, I brace myself over her while continuing to kiss her and memorizing every detail. Forever I will remember how her lips taste slightly of coconuts, how her scent of lavender washes over me, but more importantly how perfect it feels to have her pressed against me.

She moans softly, sending shivers down my spine and igniting a fire within me. I brush my thumb over her cheek, reveling in the softness of her skin beneath my touch. The fireworks continue to light up the sky, but they are nothing compared to the explosion that is happening with every one of my nerve endings everywhere she is touching me.

Her hands roam my back and hold me tightly to her like she's afraid I'm going to pull away at any moment. I've been waiting for this moment for years. One thing I know for sure, I'm not stopping now. I'm so painfully hard and I know she can feel it. What I wouldn't give to feel how soaked she is, but this isn't about sex. This is just about being close to her. Intimate.

Running one hand through her hair, and then over her shoulders to her chest, I pause. I'm waiting for her to tell me to stop, but when she deepens the kiss, I reach between us and cup her breast. We both let out a moan that makes my dick impossibly harder. I kiss down her neck to her collarbone, exploring her body and committing every tiny detail to memory. Like how she moans when I kiss the soft spot at the base of her neck and how her back bows off the dock when I pinch her hard nipple.

When I pull her shirt up desperate to find out what her tits taste like, she moans again.

"Josh..."

She cries my name in such ecstasy. But something about it pulls me from the moment. What am I doing?

Taking control, I give her a soft final kiss, drawing back. When I look into Jenna's eyes, they reflect back to me all her emotion and contentment. Wrapping my arms around her tightly, I hold on to the afterglow of the fireworks we created of our own. Then I lie down and pull her to my side.

For a few more precious moments, we lie there talking and absorbing the peace of the night, while watching the last of the firework show.

Once the fireworks are over, and the sky darkens, so does my mood. I can't believe I let myself get so carried away. Sitting up, I run a hand down my face, trying to put the wall back up that I never should have let come down.

"Let's get you back to your car." I stand and grab the blanket without even looking at her.

"Josh..."

I shake my head and silently turn away, my heart and body still feeling her even though my mind is telling me to forget it ever happened.

Jenna comes up beside me as we walk down the dock, and I finally turn to look at her. I'm met with her teary eyes, and I realize I'm going to have to explain.

"I'm sorry, Jenna. I shouldn't have let that happen."

"No," she says and puts a hand on my shoulder. "I'm glad it did."

Looking into her eyes, I can see the sincerity there.

I still can't believe she could want me. A man fifteen years older than her, someone closer to her father's age than hers.

We get in my truck, and I drive her back to her car behind the diner.

Pulling up, I shut the truck off and look at Jenna, who is just watching out the windshield.

"I'm sorry," I whisper, feeling like I'm betraying her somehow.

Jenna looks at me and places her hand on mine. "Don't be. Thank you for tonight. It was perfect."

I smile at her and brush a tear from her cheek. "Thank you for being you."

Turning away, I clear my throat, fighting the emotion that wants to make its way back.

"Text me when you get home, so I know you made it there safely. And let me know how things went with your brothers' today." I'm trying to build that wall back up between us.

"I will." She nods before getting out of my truck.

Then I watch her walk to her car and get in. She starts her car and pulls out of the parking lot in front of me. I follow her down the back road until she turns right to go home, and I have to go left to my ranch.

Taking a deep breath, I shake my head. That was way too close. No matter how hard it might be, I have to keep my distance from Jenna.

Once I arrive home, I don't even bother turning on the lights. Instead, I go straight to my room, remove my clothes, and step into the shower. The ice-cold water does nothing to calm the fire she started out there on the deck. My dick is still so damn hard hurt it hurts.

Turning the water to lukewarm, I grab some soap intent on taking care of my dick so I can concentrate on something other than what I wish would have happened tonight.

I see Jenna lying on the dock with the fireworks giving over glows of different colors. Just that image alone, has me rubbing my cock at a punishing pace. What if I hadn't stopped when I did? What if I had pushed her shirt up and gotten to taste her perfect breasts? What if I pulled those shorts down and found her soaked for me?

Running my hands down my body, I bite my lip in frustration. Jenna was right there and for a moment, I had forgotten who she was and what the consequences would be if I kept going. If I had spread her legs and pushed my hard cock inside of her, I wouldn't be doing this right now.

Screaming into the shower tile, I jerk myself harder and faster, thinking about what it would feel like to have her wrapped around me, squeezing me as we both came undone.

My body convulses as my release splashes on the shower tiles and washes down the drain. It was wrong of me to even let myself think of it and now I'm left wanting more.

I hear my phone go off, letting me know I have a text message. So, I shut the water off and step out of the shower. Wrapping a towel around my waist, I check it. Finding a message from Jenna letting me know she made it home safely.

Now I'm thinking of her at home in her pajamas and wondering if she is touching herself to images of me. And I'm hard again.

I realize the only thing that is ever going to take care of this is Jenna. No matter what I do, I can't seem to shake her. Even worse, nor do I want to.

Chapter 4
JENNA

The entire drive home all I can think about in what it felt like to have Josh kissing me, his lips on mine and his hard body caging me in. I don't think I've ever been so turned on in my life. In order to calm down enough to walk into the house and talk to my parents, I have to drive around the block twice.

"Mom? Dad?" I call out as I enter from the mudroom.

"In the kitchen," Mom calls back.

I head to the back of the house and join them. They are snacking on some baked goods, so I join them sitting on the bar stool at the kitchen island.

"So, how did the ranch tour go?" I ask.

"The property would have been beautiful in its heyday, but it's been let go. Most of the buildings, including the barn, are total tear downs. The house needs so much work to even get it livable. Not to mention it also needs a new roof. All the work it would entail completely pushes it out of their budget. Even though we spent several hours walking the property figuring out costs trying to see if we could make it work, but we just couldn't," Dad says.

"That sucks. I know they are excited to find a place."

"Yes, but it has to be the right place which takes patience," Mom says.

"Which they don't have," I say.

"That they don't. Care to watch a movie with us? Your brothers went to some bonfire after the fireworks. Oh, how was the festival? Did Josh stay?" Dad asks.

"It was fun. He did, and we went on rides and ate, did some shopping then watched the fireworks. It was fun, but we missed you guys."

"We stopped by long enough to say hello to a few people and grab some baked goods. Then we came home and watched the fireworks from the back deck. It was nice to avoid the crowds," Mom says.

"I agree. We watched from the dock of a friend of mine's lake cabin. It was really fun. But I'm going to turn down the movie. I'm exhausted and want to shower and call Sky before I go to bed." Then giving Mom and Dad both a hug and kiss, I retreat to my room and lock the door.

My room is on the other side of the house from my parents. It also has an ensuite bathroom. Mom and Dad gave me this room so I wouldn't have to share a bathroom with my brothers, but it also gives me a lot more privacy too.

First, I text Josh, so he doesn't worry.

> I made it home. My parents said most of the buildings had to be torn down on the ranch, so my brothers' passed on it.

> I'm sorry to hear that. They will find the right place soon. Glad you made it home safe.

> I had a really fun time tonight. Thank you again for spending the day with me.

The pause between his next text is so long, I think he isn't going to answer me.

> I had more fun than I should have. You don't have to thank me for spending time with you. I enjoy it. Good night, get some rest. It's been a long day.

> Good night. Dream of me.

Again, another long pause and I can imagine him shaking his head when he reads my text, and it makes me smile.

> I will be.

I don't want to ruin it, so I don't say anything else, but I call Sky.

"Hey, how was the festival?" she answers.

"My parents bailed, and I made out with someone, and I need to talk. Can I spend the night?" I ask suddenly worried about my parents overhearing any part of what I need to tell her.

"Of course. Want me to send Dash to pick you up?"

"Nope, I'm on my way. See you soon." I tell her as I pull a duffle bag from my closet and toss in some clothes and toiletries. Then I grab my phone charger and go downstairs.

"Hey, I'm heading to Sky's place for the night. She wants to have some girl talk time." I say to my parents when I get downstairs.

"Okay, sweetie, text when you get there and have fun!" Mom calls out to me, never taking her eyes off the TV.

I give them both a quick kiss on the cheek on my way out. While I'm driving over to Sky's, I decide to call Sarah and tell them everything at the same time. They are my two best friends and biggest supporters. They won't judge, and they will give me their honest opinions too.

As I pull into Sky's driveway, she greets me with a warm hug and a big smile. "Come on in, let's chat," she says, leading me to the living room. We sit on her sofa, surrounded by fluffy pillows and soft blankets.

Her husband, Dash, comes in with a bottle of wine and two wine glasses. He also hands us a box of Sky's favorite chocolates.

"You ladies need anything else?" he asks.

Sky looks at me.

"Maybe your laptop? I think we should video call Sarah in for this," I say. Dash nods and leaves to get the laptop.

Then I pull out my phone to text her, asking if she is free. Sarah texts me back immediately, saying she is going to her room so she can chat in privacy.

After Dash sets up the laptop for us, he says, "Alright, I'm going to do some ranch paperwork in the office. Call if you need anything." Then he leans down and kisses Sky. Not some quick peck on the lips, either. It's pretty hot and passionate too.

Those two are so truly in love that is makes my heart hurt. I'm hoping one day I will find that.

Once he leaves, we call Sarah, and no sooner is she connected than Sky turns to me, "Okay, spill. What happened at the festival?"

Taking a deep breath, I tell them everything. I recount how my parents bailed, and Josh and I had spent the majority of the day together, going on rides, eating food, and shopping. As I talk, I can feel my face turning red with embarrassment.

After I tell them about the Ferris wheel and the almost kiss which follows, I get squeals from them. I then tell them about the fireworks on Sarah's in-law's deck and the mini make out season, ending with the text we shared once I got home.

Of course, I have to admit how I've had a crush on Josh since I was sixteen and how over the last two years, it's developed into something more. Then I wait for their opinions.

"When you say father's best friend. How old is he?" Sarah asks.

"He's thirty-eight, fifteen years older than me."

"Okay, I'm only going to ask this because I love you. He hasn't touched you before tonight? Or made a move before?" Sky asks.

I know she wants to know this because I've known this man almost all my life.

"Not once. He moved away when I was sixteen, and then I didn't see him until my high school graduation. He followed my dad here and didn't start having weekly dinners with us until about a year ago," I tell them.

"Do you have any photos?" Sarah asks. I pull a few from my phone that we took today and show them.

"Damn, he's good looking for an older guy. But don't tell my husband I said that," Sarah says.

Her husband Mac knows she loves him. They have been dancing around each other since they were teens, and Sky got to watch the whole thing. I'm a bit jealous I didn't meet them until later, but I still got to see them finally give in to their love.

"So, what is holding you back?" Sky asks.

"Well, it's him fighting moving forward. Wondering how my dad would take it once he found out, and what people will think when they know..."

"First, screw everyone else. Don't ruin your chance at happiness because of what other people *might* think," Sarah says.

"I have to agree with her there," Sarah says. "From the sound of things, it seems like your dad is the biggest issue here. Josh is holding back because your father is his best friend. You are hesitant because it's your dad."

"Your dad is going to love you no matter what. He will eventually forgive you, and you will be okay. It's Josh that has the most to lose here. Their friendship might not recover," Sky says.

I know she's right. Sighing heavily, I lean back on the couch, feeling overwhelmed by my conflicting feelings. On the one hand, I can't deny the intense attraction I feel towards Josh. On the other hand, I don't want to jeopardize his relationship with my dad or have our own relationship scrutinized by others.

"I don't know what to do," I admit, looking at my friends for answers that I know they can't give me. "I feel like I'm stuck between a rock and a hard place."

"Sadly, this is a situation where you have to take a step back and let Josh make his choice. He has the most to lose, and he has to be the one to choose to move forward," Sky says.

"That doesn't mean you can't let him know that you want this and that you are there for him. Personally, I say take the chance. I was in your shoes with Mac, and we lost so much time because we danced around each other. Stop waiting," Sarah says.

"I agree. Make sure he knows you want this, but don't push too hard. He has to make the choice," Sky adds.

"And how do I do that?" "You could always take a dinner over to his place. Say you didn't want to eat by yourself because your parents aren't home. Then you two are alone at his place and see where it goes," Sky says.

The idea isn't half bad, and it gives me something to think about. We stay up and talk and catch up with each other for a bit longer. As the night grows later, I realize just how much I have missed my friends and how much I value their advice.

Once we hang up and finish our conversation with Sarah, Sky gives me a hug. Then Dash and her take me out to the loft above the garage.

"This way you can have your own space to think. Come back to the main house for breakfast whenever you get up," Sky says before leaving me with my thoughts.

This is the loft Sky stayed in when she worked for Dash. It took her a while before she realized the man everyone called The Beast was really her ex-boyfriend. He had been hiding in plain sight with long hair and a beard. They have been inseparable ever since.

After I change into my pajamas, I flop down on the bed. I want some time alone with Josh. Though I'm still worried what people will think or say behind my back. It is a small town, and I've made it a point to get to know everyone. After all, that was the entire big reason I've taken the job waiting tables at the diner. What will they think of me dating someone so much older? Do I care what they think? What will they say? What could they do to me?

Before I make a move like bringing Josh dinner, I have to decide what I want. If I make such a bold move, I need to know for sure that I am all in.

Chapter 5
Josh

It's been a few days since the July 4th festival and I'm back over at Evan's house helping him fix a classic Chevy Impala that he just bought. We're going over it and making a list of everything that needs to be done and parts that he needs to get, which to be honest, is a lot.

I think this car is more of something to keep him busy in his retirement. Not that he's retired too much, from what Janet says.

"Sorry for bailing on you at the festival. But I wanted to thank you for keeping an eye on Jenna when we weren't there," he says.

When guilt starts to churn in my belly, I shake my head, trying to dispel the feeling. "No worries, man. Jenna's fun to be around and I had a blast hanging out with her and watching the fireworks."

At the mention of fireworks, the images of our make-out session on the dock fill my head. Those images are never far from my thoughts and right now is the worst possible time to think about them. Getting hard while I'm talking to my best friend about his daughter is not cool.

Evans nods at my words, and his weathered face creases into a smile. "Glad to hear it. That girl's the light of my life."

I smile back, feeling a warmth spread through my chest. Evan may be a hard man to those who don't know him, but there's a softness in his heart that he reserves for his family. Right now, he considers me family, but if he ever found out about what happened on that dock, I'd be dead to him. Maybe even physically dead, too.

"How is Jenna doing, really? She's been spending a lot of time over at Sky's place, so I haven't been able to talk to her too much," he says.

This is the first I'm hearing about her being over at Sky's place. I guess I always assumed she was home if she wasn't working, which is crazy. Of course, she has friends and a social life. She's twenty-three, why wouldn't she being going out and having fun? But the thought of her going out with another guy doesn't sit well with me either.

"Well, when I was with her the other day, she seemed to be doing well. She still likes her time at the diner, but from the way she talks, I think she just likes the social aspect of talking to everyone while she's there."

Evans nods slowly, his eyes studying me closely. "That's good to hear. I just want her to be happy, you know? These last few days she has been really cheerful like a weight has been lifted off her shoulders. Whatever you said to her really seemed to help."

I nod, feeling a heaviness settle in my stomach. How am I supposed to tell him I'm the one making his daughter happy? That we've been seeing each other behind his back and that I can't get enough of her? The answer is I can't. Plain and simple. So I go for a version of the truth.

"We talked about her book like you asked. She is stuck on the ending of it, how to bring it to a conclusion. I suggested she put it away for a few weeks or so and enjoy the summer, then go back to it and see what comes up."

"That's a good idea. She needs to get out more, anyway. I hate to say it with her being my daughter, but she needs to date. She hasn't been out with a guy since she got home from college and broke up with that college boyfriend of hers. I want her to find a good man, someone who will support her dream of writing even if she isn't making money at it. But she can't do that if she doesn't get out of the house," he says.

My heart sinks at the mention of Jenna seeing someone. Just the thought of her being with another guy makes me feel sick to my stomach. But I couldn't let Evans know that, so I put on my best poker face. "Well, maybe she just hasn't found the right guy yet. I'm sure she will eventually. Let's be honest, she probably won't tell you she is even dating anyone until it's more serious." I force a smile, hoping it looks genuine.

Evans chuckles. "Yeah, you're probably right about that. Girls can be pretty secretive about those things. At least to their parents."

As we continue to work on the car, my mind keeps drifting back to Jenna. I know it's wrong, but I can't help the way I feel. She's smart, funny, beautiful, and I enjoy every minute I get to spend with her. But then the reality sets in - she's my best friend's daughter, and it's wrong to feel this way about her.

Trying to push these thoughts aside, I focus on the task at hand. Evans is telling me about his plans to take his wife on a cruise for their anniversary. As he talks about her, I can see the love shining in his eyes. In spite of myself, I can't stop the pang of envy for what they have. It's been years since I've been in any kind of relationship and seeing how happy they are only makes the loneliness sting that much more.

When we finally finish up working on the car, Evan claps me on the back, snapping me out of my thoughts. "Thanks for your help with the car, Josh. I'll let you get back to your day."

Nodding my head, I try to appear nonchalant as I say my goodbyes. But as I walk away, my thoughts drift back to Jenna. The memory of the last time we were together sends a wave of desire crashing through my body. It's like an addiction, one that I can't shake off. Nor do I want to.

It's past noon and I haven't eaten since breakfast, so without a second thought I decide to stop and grab lunch at the diner.

It has everything to do with my rumbling stomach and nothing to do with the chance of seeing Jenna while she is working.

It's past the normal lunch rush, so I'm able to snag a parking spot in the front of the diner. When I walk in, Jenna is cleaning off a table by the door.

"Josh, good to see you," she says with a smile.

"Hey Jenna. Just got done helping your dad with that car he recently purchased and realized I hadn't had lunch." I say lamely, like I need an excuse to be here.

"Mom didn't feed you?" She asks me as she walks the pile of dishes toward the counter and sets them down. Then, grabbing a towel and spray, she comes back to the table to clean it.

"She wasn't there. Evan said she was out at some fundraiser for the library. At least that's what I think I heard."

"Well, grab a table anywhere." She says as she finishes wiping the table down.

"What section is yours?"

Pointing, she says, "Right side over there." Then she grabs the dishes from the counter and takes them to the back.

I pick up a menu and sit at a table in the corner, giving me a view of the diner, and to be honest, a view of wherever she ends up.

As I peruse the menu, my mind wanders back to Jenna on the dock the other night. I try to push the thoughts away, knowing that it's wrong to have these feelings for her. But like a magnet, those thoughts keep coming no matter how much I resist.

Just then, Jenna comes over to take my order. Her smile is infectious, and I feel warmth spread through my body as she stands there in front of me.

"Hey Josh, what can I get for you?" she asks, her voice soft and captivating.

"Just a burger and fries, please," I reply, trying to keep my voice steady.

"Burger with ketchup and mayo, no mustard, extra cheese, and sweet tea. You got it," she says.

"You remember all your customer's orders?" I ask impressed she got my order right.

"Only the regulars and the cute cowboys I can't seem to get out of my head," she says.

Before I can even get a word out, she spins and goes into the kitchen.

I'm sure I look like an idiot sitting there with my mouth open in complete shock. A quick look around the diner proves no one was in earshot. There is only one older couple at a table in the opposite corner, and no way should they hear anything.

I can feel the heat rising to my cheeks as I try to process what Jenna just said. Did she really just call me cute? My mind is racing as I try to come up with a response, but before I can even open my mouth, she's back with my drink.

As she sets the cup in front of me, her fingers lightly brush against mine, sending a jolt of electricity through my body.

"I'll have your food out soon," she says, her voice low and sexy.

Once again, she goes back to the kitchen, leaving me alone with my thoughts.

My thoughts fixate on the way her fingers felt against mine, the rightness of it. What would happen if I was brave enough to act on these feelings?

Unable to take my eyes off of her, I watch as she brings the food to the other table, stopping and chatting to them. She is smiling and laughing, and the couple seems to know her, and I wonder if people come back just to visit her. I know that is the biggest draw that brought me here today instead of heading home and grabbing some cold leftovers.

Jenna goes into the kitchen, coming back with my order, and sets the plate in front of me. "Enjoy, cowboy," she says with a wink before gliding sexily back to the kitchen.

My heart is beating so fast I can't even concentrate on my food.

When I take a bite of my burger, the taste is lost on me. All I can think about now is Jenna. I can still feel her soft hair in my hands and her curves pressed against me.

Then, as I take a sip of my sweet tea, I catch her looking at me from across the diner. Our eyes meet, and once again the heat rises to my cheeks and other places. But this time, I don't look away.

Jenna walks over to my table and takes a seat across from me. "Is everything okay with your food?" she asks, but her eyes tell me there's more to her visit than just checking on my meal.

"Yeah, it's great. Thanks," I reply, trying to keep my composure.

She leans in a little closer, her eyes never leaving mine. "You know, Josh, I've been thinking about that night on the dock a lot lately," she says softly.

My heart wants to be out of my chest at her words.

"I have too," I reply, my voice low and husky.

Desire is clear in her eyes as she studies my face for just a moment. But she doesn't get a chance to reply because Austin calls to her from the kitchen. She smiles at me and turns to see what Austin wants.

Quickly, I finish my meal, pay my bill, and leave a generous tip for Jenna. As I walk out of the diner, I see her standing at the door to the kitchen, watching me leave. Our eyes meet for a brief moment before I turn and walk away, my mind reeling with thoughts of her.

I know I need to stop these feelings before they get out of hand, but it's easier said than done. Though I wonder hopefully and somewhat urgently, if there's a chance for us, even just a small one.

Chapter 6
JENNA

Seeing Josh at the diner yesterday was nice. It was so easy to flirt, and I felt at ease around him. Though I know I need to be careful about flirting in public like that. I know how worried he is about things getting back to my dad.

Today I'm out looking at another ranch with my brothers. Mom and Dad couldn't make it, but promised if they thought this was it, they'd take a look tomorrow. It's been a while since I've had alone time with my brothers, so it's good to catch up.

They have been talking about buying a ranch and running it together since they were in high school, maybe even before that. So I love being with them as they check out a possible ranch.

Driving down the dirt road that leads to the ranch, I listen as my brothers make plans. They talk about the cattle they would raise and the crops they would plant. In my mind's eye, I could see them working together, making their dream a reality. It makes me happy to see them so enthusiastic about something.

When we arrive at the ranch house, their real estate agent, who goes by Maverick, is waiting for us on the porch.

"Hey guys, this place is bigger than the last one we saw, and it needs work, but I think it could be the one for you. It's not officially on the market yet, so you are the first to see it," he says.

It's on the same side of the lake as our parents' house and the home is built on one corner of it. It looks like a Texas farmhouse and is in decent condition.

"Over the years, the home has had some remodels done. Even though it was built in the 1920s, it's up to code with new electricity and plumbing put in two years ago. I'll let you take a look around and let me know what you think," Maverick says.

"What do you think, Jenna? Would a woman like to live here one day?" Asher asks.

"The way she is going, maybe this should be her house, and we just set up on the other three corners of the property," Zach jokes.

"That's not a bad idea. You are always welcome if you want to get out on your own," Asher says.

Finn nods his head, "Yeah, it would be great."

"Thank you, guys, but that's not really where my heart is. But I'll keep it open as an option. Never know where life might take me. Though for sure, I might come out here to write."

"Whenever, you want, you don't need an invitation." Asher pulls me against him for a side hug.

"The kitchen is a good size. Appliances will get you through," I say, "but a woman will want to update them. Hardwood floors are nice, plan for rugs, especially in the winter. The dining room is big enough for the whole family. The laundry room leads outside so you guys can come in, strip there and not track dirt throughout the house. There is even an office space down here. So far, so good."

I switch gears and we go upstairs to look at the four bedrooms and two bathrooms. Other than some paint on the walls, it's good to go.

"Why don't you guys go look at the barn and bunkhouse out back?" Maverick says. "My wife is calling, and I'll join you and tell you more about the land in a few."

"So, what's new with you? Seeing anyone?" Finn winks at me as we walk down to the barn.

He is such a playboy, but I love him all the same. "No, nothing new. Just focusing on my writing and trying to get published."

Asher chuckles. "That's our Jenna, always chasing her dreams."

I smile at him, feeling grateful for my brothers and their unwavering support.

"Can I ask you guys a question, though?" I want to get an opinion from them because I know they won't push for more info than I'm ready to divulge.

"Always. What's up?" Zach asks, and they all stop to look at me as we reach the barn.

"What would you think of me dating an older guy?" I ask.

"Anyone we know?" Asher looks at me, studying my face.

I shake my head. "No, just in general. I met a guy recently who's slightly older than me and I'm curious what you guys think."

"How much older?" Zach asks.

"I don't know. Fifteen years or so?" I'm cringing, hoping they don't bring up Josh.

Finn smirks. "Well, older guys are more experienced, right? Maybe he can show you a thing or two."

I roll my eyes at him. "That's not what I meant. I just don't want you guys to think I'm making a mistake or anything."

Zach puts a hand on my shoulder. "Jenna, we trust your judgment. If you think he's a good guy, then we're happy for you."

Asher nods in agreement.

"Yeah, we just want you to be happy. Age shouldn't matter as long as he treats you right," he says with a smile.

There is such a sense of relief which washes over me at their words. I know I shouldn't let their opinions dictate my decisions, but their support means everything to me.

"Thanks, guys, I really appreciate it," I say, feeling grateful for their love and understanding.

"Now, let's take a look at this barn," I say, stepping inside.

"It's small, we'd have to add on," Finn says.

"But there is an office in the back too, so that's a bonus," I say as we move on to the bunkhouse.

"Small barn but large bunkhouse. This is more than we'd need, probably ever." Asher says as we look at the ten bunk beds that would sleep twenty people. The kitchen is larger than the main house, and there are three bathrooms.

"It would be nice to update it though," Zach says.

We all agree. The floors are fake wood, and the walls are in desperate need of a paint job, and it would be nice for them to have a sitting or TV area.

"Fifteen years, huh?" Asher says, standing beside me.

"Think that's too old?" I ask him.

"I think anything over twenty years would be too old. You don't want them to die when you are in your thirties. You want to spend time with them and enjoy life."

"I'm not sure if I'd date anyone over ten years older than me. I don't think they could keep up," Finn smirks.

"Well, maybe you need to slow down. But you guys have to think about it from the other end. How much younger than you would you date?" I shove Finn with my shoulder.

"Huh, okay. Seven years for me because that puts her at eighteen and I'm not into the whole jailbait thing." Zach tells me as we head back to the main house.

"Have you seen the eighteen-year-old's now? I don't think you could keep up with them." Finn says, knocking off Zach's cowboy hat, but he manages to catch it before it hits the ground.

We all laugh as we continue our way back to the main house. Though I must admit that I'm feeling relieved that my brothers are supportive of me potentially dating an older man. It's not that I need their approval, but it certainly makes the decision easier knowing that they're on board with it.

I'm still unsure if I'm ready to push Josh or not, but knowing I have my brother's support with the age gap makes the choice easier.

Once we're back to the house, Maverick greets us with a smile. "So, what do you guys think?"

"It seems good. The barn is a bit small, and the bunkhouse needs work. Talk to us about the land." Asher says any hint of playfulness was gone.

"The land goes for miles. Perfect for hunting and fishing. And the best part is, it's completely private. No neighbors for miles."

We all gather around as Maverick shows us a map of the land. It's vast, with fields and forests, and a river running through it.

"It's beautiful," Asher says, his eyes scanning the map.

"And a great place to get inspiration for your writing," Finn adds, nudging my arm.

I nod in agreement, taking in the beauty of the land. "It definitely has potential," I say.

They talk about price, and Asher pulls out his phone, and the frown on his face indicates that for some reason, this isn't the one either. The other guys pick up on it too and we head out to the truck to go home.

"What was wrong with it?" I ask as we drive away.

"The price they wanted was more than double per acre than anything we have seen. Even though we'll offer them fair market value, I'm willing to bet they think we are low balling them and they'll walk away," Asher says.

We get home and they go to talk to Mom and Dad while I go to my room and get ready for work. Normally I'm happy to be at work and see everyone who stops in, but today my mind keeps going back to Josh. Do I really want to commit to making the next move, putting my heart on the line and facing possible rejection and losing him forever?

I have stayed away, but that was before I knew what it felt like to be kissed and held by him. Now I don't think I can go back.

"Jenna, you okay, Hun?" Austin comes up behind me.

"Yeah, why?" I ask, trying to focus on my job.

"You have been standing there staring into space and Mr. Jones has been trying to flag you down for a few minutes now," she says.

"Shoot," I say, looking his way and smiling.

"Go help him, then come back, and we can chat," she says.

Austin is the diner owner's niece and only a few years older than me. When the last diner owner went full on stalker to my friend Sarah, he found himself in a jail cell. Not too long after, Austin moved to town to take over for her aunt. Austin's sister, Natalie, followed, but she didn't work here long once she met her husband Royce. Now that her baby was born, she's been a ranch wife and loving it.

I get Mr. Jones his refill, and his check before finding Austin in the back.

"What do you think about me dating a guy who is fifteen years older than me?" I come right out with it.

"Anyone I know?" She asks like my brothers did.

I shake my head. "No, just someone I met recently. He's incredibly sweet and we have a real connection, but the age difference is just..." I trail off, unsure of how to finish that sentence.

"Well, I don't think age should play much a part of it as long as both people are over eighteen. It should be about how he treats you and how he makes you feel. And how you feel when you are around him. He should help you be a better version of yourself. Personally, I think an older man would be able to do that much better than a younger one," she says.

"I couldn't agree more."

Austin smiles at me and pats my arm. "Then go for it, girl. Don't let the age difference hold you back from something that could be great."

I nod, feeling a renewed sense of determination. Maybe it was time for me to take that leap and make my move with Josh. After all, what did I have to lose? Things might be awkward for a bit with my parents, but I know we eventually my dad will come around.

I'm going to go for it. If I don't, I will always regret it and will wonder what if. I don't want to live with that.

Chapter 7
JOSH

I love working on this land and with the animals that live on it. It's hard but rewarding work. What I hate is after a long hard day having to come inside and cook something for myself.

Janet has been great at stuffing my freezer with casseroles I can just pop in the oven. She was horrified to find most days I was living on frozen dinners from the store. Usually, Janet and Jenna will make several meals and send them home with me on Sundays. But now I'm starting to wonder if Jenna had more to do with it than I realized.

Sadly, I ate the last of the casseroles yesterday and haven't had a chance to run to the store, so I don't even have a frozen dinner waiting for me. I'm covered in dirt, need a shower and a quick glance at my fridge reveals nothing. I guess it's going to have to be peanut butter and Jelly sandwiches for dinner.

But first I need a shower. Once I make it to my room upstairs, I strip out of my clothes. I'll pick them up later, but right now I am looking forward to the hot water.

When I step into the shower, the hot water cascades over my body, washing away the dirt and grime of the day. My muscles relax as the tension of the day is fades away.

The moment I close my eyes, I see Jenna on the dock again. I can feel her against my body, and the peace I was feeling a moment ago is long gone. I quickly shower, dry off, and get dressed. After picking up my dirty clothes, I go down to the kitchen to wolf down my peanut butter and jelly sandwiches.

No sooner do I start the load of laundry than there is a knock on my door. Since I'm not expecting anyone, I hesitantly make my way to the door. I'm shocked to find Jenna standing there with a few shopping bags in her hands.

"Jenna, everything okay?" I ask like an idiot because I have no idea why she is here.

"Yep. Mom and Dad have been out with friends every night this week. My brothers never eat at home anymore and I'm tired of eating by myself. So I picked up stuff to make lasagna and decided we should have dinner together."

I hesitate for a moment, still feeling a bit unsettled by the memory of Jenna on the dock. Though I don't want to turn her away, the lasagna sounds better than peanut butter and jelly. I should send her home and get rid of the temptation to take this further, but ultimately I can't say no to a home-cooked meal and the company of someone I care about.

"Sure, that sounds great," I say, stepping aside to let Jenna into my home. As she heads to the kitchen, I'm noticing how good she looks. Her long, dark brown hair is pulled back in a messy bun, and she's wearing a pair of denim shorts and a red tank top that show off her toned body.

"What can I do to help?" I ask, following her into the kitchen.

"Nothing. I know you have been out working all day. Sit down and keep me company." She nods to the stool at the kitchen island.

Taking a seat at the table, I watch Jenna bustle around the kitchen, pulling out ingredients and mixing them together with ease. She's always been a natural in the kitchen, a talent she inherited from her mother.

As she works, it's interesting how at home she is in my kitchen. This isn't the first time she's been here, just the first time she's been here alone. Though I can't shake the feeling of how much I really like her being here in my space and cooking for me. Nor do I want to because it seems right.

My mind starts to wonder what it would be like to come in from a long day like today and walk into the house to find her cooking for me. Being able to go to her, hold her in my arms, and kiss her. Maybe even have her join me in the shower.

"Did you like the garlic bread I made for you last time?" she asks, breaking me out of my daydream.

"The one with the Italian seasoning and cheese? Yes, very much."

"Perfect, I will make it again." She pulls a loaf of bread from one of the bags.

As Jenna slices the bread, I notice the way her fingers move with precision and grace, working the knife like an artist with a paintbrush. She catches me staring and gives me a small smile, her hazel eyes locking with mine.

All this time, I keep thinking about how good she looks, how much I want to touch her, to kiss her. When she turns to grab a pot from the pantry, I get a glimpse of the curve of her ass.

My thoughts quickly become more explicit, imagining all the things I would like to do to her in the heat of the moment. How badly I want to push her up against the counter and feel her pressed to me again.

Instead, I quickly shake my head, trying to clear my mind of these erotic thoughts. I can't let myself be consumed by this attraction.

"So, how have you been?" I ask, needing to focus on something more mundane to distract myself.

"Alright. I went with my brothers to look at a ranch yesterday. They liked it but the seller was asking double per acre than anyone else in the area. They put in a fair market value offer and were turned down immediately. Asher says the wife is probably making him sell, but he doesn't want to," she shrugs.

I make a note to go visit my neighbor Willy. He was talking about possibly selling last time we talked but made it clear he won't be selling to the land developers that are sniffing around town. But I don't want to get Jenna or her brothers' hopes up, so I'm not going to say anything until I talk to him.

"They will find the right place eventually."

I get up and start setting the table as she pulls the lasagna out of the oven.

Jenna places the lasagna on the table, and the smell of the hot, cheesy dish fills the room. We both sit down and start to eat, the conversation picking up again.

"Wow, this is amazing. Better than I remember," I say between bites.

She might think I'm just saying that, but I'm not. She is an amazing cook and going to make some lucky bastard a great wife. It just can't be me. During dinner, we don't run out of things to talk about. Everything from our favorite TV shows to what is going on at my ranch.

She shares some of the town gossip, which is more fun than it should be.

"You know Mr. Perkin's wife caught him walking around the house wearing her black heels? The way she was going on and on, you'd have thought Satan himself made an appearance. She has been praying nonstop. They had to kick her out of church the other night so they could close up."

"Oh man, he's my banker," l say laughing. In order to try to get that image from my mind, I shake my head.

"Mr. Owen's wife ran off with some male stripper she met on her last trip to Las Vegas. Apparently, they went for their anniversary, and both agreed the other could hire a stripper. Now Mr. Owen is on a rampage about how men don't need to be in the stripper business and how they pray on lonely old women." She giggles as she relates the gossip.

"Yet, if he had been paying attention to her, she wouldn't have been lonely. I also know he's been sleeping with his secretary on the side," I tell her. "Did you know that he's the slime lawyer who has been working with the property developers no one wants in town?"

"The entire town knows. It's why Mrs. Owen was so eager to get some action of her own. Now he's complaining how she's getting half of everything, saying the stripper will leave her and take half of her half," Jenna adds.

I watch her as she talks, and it doesn't go unnoticed by me how easy she is to talk to and how natural having dinner and catching up with her is. She is smiling down at her plate and when she looks up, our eyes meet.

The intensity in her gaze is enough to make my heart skip a beat, causing me to lose track of the conversation. She smiles shyly at me, and there's no way I could do anything else, but smile at her too.

She sets her fork down and takes a deep breath. "Why do you keep fighting this?"

Not accusing, but genuinely wanting an answer. I could sit here and play dumb, but she's too smart for that. Plus, she deserves an answer. After everything, I at least owe her that.

"Because your father is my best friend, and I can't do that to him."

"My dad wants us both to be happy." I know she's right, but it's so much more than that. It's about loyalty and the breaking of trust that would occur. I don't know how to put it into words for her, so I say nothing.

"So, all this has just been one sided? A quick fling, a slip up? I was in the wrong place at the wrong time? There are no actual feelings for me?" The hurt is clear in her voice and on her face.

I can't answer her because doing so would be saying she was anything but. She's all I ever wanted, but telling her that gives her a kind of hope I can't give her. "I'm sorry," I say softly, wanting her to know she isn't just a fling or a mistake. That she means more than that.

She looks away, her face still a mask of hurt and frustration. Standing abruptly, she starts to collect the plates, her head turned from me.

I sit in silence, my heart heavy. Even though I want to say something, anything to make it all better, but the words just won't come.

She sets the plates on the counter, then turns to the door and gathers her things.

As she reaches for the doorknob, I stand up and grab her by the arm, forcing her to turn around to face me. The hurt and anger in her eyes are almost more than I can bear.

Yet any words I thought about saying are gone. Nothing comes out.

I let go of her arm, and she turns back for the door. I want to say something, but instead I just watch her leave.

My heart is heavy as I watch her go, wondering if this is the last time I'll ever see her like this, with her walls down.

I know what I should do, what I should say. But I'm too afraid of the consequences. Of losing her, of losing her father's friendship, of losing everything that's safe and familiar.

But the reality is, I already lost her. I've been holding onto something that's already gone.

Standing, I walk to the door, opening it and stepping out into the cool night air. As much as I want to go after her, I know it's better to leave it be. I watch her drive down the driveway and stay on the porch. Staring after her. Long after her headlights are gone.

She deserves better.

And even if it breaks my heart, I have to do what's best for her.

Chapter 8
JENNA

It's been a few days since Josh let me walk out of his house with nothing more than an 'I'm sorry.' I hate to admit I haven't really left my room other than to go to work. Though I have been busy ready about fictional men who stop at nothing for the women they love. Going as far as to kidnap them, to have them in their lives.

Is that too much to ask for? Someone who loved me so much that they can't stand to be away from me. So they commit a little kidnapping to be with me.

Experiencing those heroines falling in love helps hide my own pain of rejection and for a little while I can forget all about Josh. Then night comes and as I lie in bed, I keep seeing that dinner being played out over and over again until I pass out from exhaustion. Then my dreams are filled with what would have happened that night on the dock if we hadn't stopped.

Then I wake up feeling hot and bothered. The image of Josh's lips on mine was still fresh in my mind, even though it was just a dream.

So, I'd drown myself in another book. But reality was a far cry from the books I was reading. Josh had made it clear that he did not feel the same way about me, and it hurt. The pain was a constant reminder of my embarrassment, thinking he had any feelings for me.

Sky thinks he has feelings, but he is just scared to admit them. Maybe Sarah agrees with him, but I just don't know. I think I have to believe it was all one sided, and he doesn't have feelings for me if I have any chance of moving on with my life.

Today, my brothers have friends over to my parents, and we are all out back by the pool enjoying the hot day. To get myself out of my funk, I'm going to do some reading in the sun and work on my tan. Some Vitamin D might do me some good.

Everyone is splashing around the pool and having fun while they're grilling some burgers for lunch. Asher brought be one telling me to eat, and Finn keeps bringing me bottles of water to drink. I think Mom and Dad told them to keep an eye on me since I was actually out of my room today.

After reading a few chapters, I set the book down and watch the guys play some water volleyball. It doesn't escape me that my brothers' friends all check me out every chance they get. This black lace bikini always turns heads, but I wear it for me, because I feel the most confident in it.

Taking a drink of my water, I notice one of my brother's friends, Liam, watching me. He's always been a little flirty with me, but I've never taken it seriously. He's just a friend of my brothers, nothing more.

He smiles at me, but I don't react. Thankfully, Asher's attention is away from me and back to the game. Lying back down, I close my eyes to soak up the sun. No sooner than I get comfortable, a shadow blocks my sun. I open my eyes to find Josh, and he doesn't look happy.

"Josh?" I was shocked to see him.

"Cover up," he says, tossing a towel on me.

Sitting up, I wrap the towel around me, confused as to why Josh is here and why he's acting so cold towards me. He doesn't say anything else, just stands there with his arms crossed and a scowl on his face.

"Is everything okay?" I finally ask, hoping for some sort of explanation as to why he's here and why he seems upset.

"No, everything is not okay," he finally responds, his voice tight with anger as he glares over at Liam.

I follow his gaze and find my brother staring back at what is going on as well, even though they are out of hearing distance.

Turning back, I find Josh staring at me. "You didn't want me. You can't have it both ways," I say.

"I want you more than I should," Josh responds. His steel blue eyes soften slightly. "And seeing you here, with him, wearing that... it's driving me crazy." He gestures towards Liam, who is now talking with my brothers on the other side of the pool.

My heart races at his words, unsure of what to make of them. "What do you mean?" I ask, needing clarification.

"It means that I was an idiot to let you walk out of my house like that the other night," he says, his eyes filled with regret. "I've been kicking myself ever since."

My heart swells at his confession, and I feel a glimmer of hope that maybe, just maybe, there's a chance for us. Though I try to keep my composure, not wanting to seem too eager or desperate.

"You going to keep fighting this? Keep hurting both of us?" I ask, needing to know if there is action behind his words.

There is a possessive look in his eyes, and he takes a step toward me. I can feel my heart about racing out of my chest as he moves closer.

"Dinner at my place tonight. Bring a bag for the weekend."

Before I can say anything else, he walks back into the house.

I can hardly believe what just happened. Josh actually admitted to having feelings for me and even invited me to dinner at his place. My heart is racing with anticipation, but also with a tinge of nervousness. What if this is all a mistake, and he changes his mind again? I shake my head, trying to push away the negative thoughts and focus on the possibility of something more with Josh.

Sitting up, I swing my legs over the side of the lounger, tightening the towel around me as my brother swims over toward me. Their friends are sitting there watching and I know they saw the whole thing but didn't get to hear any of it.

"What was that about?" Asher asks when he reaches me.

Well, I can tell him mostly the truth and just leave out certain bits.

"He saw your friends drooling over me and gave me a modesty lecture. Told me to cover up."

At my words, Finn turns around to glare at the other guys, who quickly look away.

"I'm going to head inside. I have plans this weekend. I need to get ready, anyway."

"Going to Sky's place again?" Zach asks.

Well, it's as good a cover as any. Guess I need to call her and tell her. I never did ask a friend to cover for me while I was somewhere else in high school so I can get the full experience now.

When I get inside, I find Josh talking with my parents in the kitchen and his eyes are on me. My parents' backs are turned, so I smirk and drop my towel, giving him a full view of the bikini he just told me to cover up.

He rolls his eyes to the ceiling like he is saying a prayer before they land back on me.

"I'm going to my room, and then I'm heading to dinner at Sky's. I'll probably stay the weekend there and help out some." I tell my parents.

"Okay, sweetheart, give her a hug for me," Mom says.

"I will," I say, leaving the kitchen.

Not only can I feel Josh's eyes on me, but when he gets a full view of my thong bikini bottom, I can hear the cussing as I go upstairs.

"You let her wear shit like that?" I hear Josh say to my parents.

"I'm not thrilled with it, but she is an adult. We can't really stop her," Dad says.

Satisfied with myself, a big smile on my face, I run to my room. As soon as I shut the door, I get a text.

> You are playing with fire, you little tease.

> It's about time I get a reaction out of you.

> Don't wear that scrap of fabric you call a bathing suit or anything like it in front of any other guys.

> I guess that depends on how this week-end goes.

> Don't test me, Jenna. I'm barely hanging on by a thread. I'm going home now. Don't make me wait long.

> I'm packing. See you soon.

After grabbing a duffle bag, I call Sky and Sarah. I had been texting them the last few days, and they were up to date on what happened at the dinner at Josh's place.

"OMG guys!" I try to keep my voice down when they answer.

"What happened? Spill all the details!" Sarah exclaims eagerly.

"Josh just admitted he has feelings for me and invited me to dinner at his place tonight," I reply. Though I'm still in disbelief at what had just happened.

"No way! That's amazing!" Sky chimes in.

"I know! I'm so excited but also kind of nervous," I admit, feeling a sense of vulnerability about the possibility of opening myself up to Josh again.

"Girl! I knew he had feelings for you!" Sky says.

"Well, I also had to tell my parents I was staying at your place, so heads up, cover for me because he told me to pack a bag for the weekend. So can you do that for me with my parents if they call?"

Both girls squeal so loud I have to pull the phone away from my ear.

"Just go with the flow and enjoy the moment," Sarah advises. "And don't forget to pack some sexy outfits for the weekend!"

I laugh nervously. "I'll keep that in mind," I say, feeling my cheeks flush with embarrassment at the thought of wearing something like that in front of Josh. But at the same time, the idea of being desired by him is thrilling.

He's been fighting me for so long I don't know if he will be ready to take that step, but it can't hurt. I pack my sexiest PJs. Super short cotton shorts and a lace see through tank top. Then I add my cutest bras and underwear and some sexy clothes and another bathing suit. I'm not going down without a fight.

Then I change into a pair of shorts that have rips in the back, showing just a hint of my ass. I bought these specifically to get Josh's attention a few months ago and have only worn them around him. Pairing them with a crop top and sandals and I'm almost ready to go. I pull my hair into a messy bun, and take a deep breath, going downstairs. My parents are sitting in the living room, watching TV.

"Hey Mom, Dad, I'm heading out now. Have a great weekend," I say, giving them each a hug and a kiss on the cheek.

"Be safe and have fun," Mom says.

Thankfully, they don't pay me much attention. Making my way to the front door, I step outside, feeling the warmth of the sun on my skin. My nerves are hitting me in full force because the possibilities for this weekend are endless.

This is either the start of something between us or we are going to go down in flames. There will be no in-between.

Chapter 9
JOSH

As soon as I get home, I run upstairs and take a quick shower, changing into a nice pair of jeans and a button-down shirt.

What the hell was I thinking?

For sure, I can tell you I was thinking with the wrong damn part of my body. But seeing her stretched out in the sun with her golden skin on display, I was unprepared to see her incredible body. She looked absolutely fucking gorgeous in that lace bikini on the lounge chair and something inside me snapped, seeing the other guys eyeballing her.

Now, I can't stop thinking about her. Her curves, her gorgeous breasts, and her soft skin. She has no idea how close I came to kissing her and claiming her as mine right then and there in front of her mom, dad, and her brothers. That would have been a disaster and would ruin everything.

Her brother's friends were outright ogling her. How her brothers didn't pick up on it, I have no idea. Now that I think about it, I'm not sure how I had the restraint to keep my hands off of her. Especially when the little tease went upstairs showing off her tight ass in her thong bikini. Then a chilling thought crosses my mind. Maybe she was trying to get the guy's attention since I kept pushing her away.

Even if that's the case, it's not going to happen. Even though I know this isn't right and that I should not have her here for the weekend, but if she's here I can keep an eye on her. I'll know she's safe and not showing off for other guys.

Going into the kitchen, I pull out some steaks and get them marinating. Just as I get the potatoes in the oven to cook, my phone goes off. For a heart wrenching moment, I think it's Jenna coming to her senses and canceling because her brother's idiot friends asked her out.

I know they won't get far as I'd be there to rip her from any kind of date. If one of those boys thinks that they can touch someone as beautiful, kind, and pure as Jenna, they're very much mistaken. But when I reach for my phone, I see it's her dad, which just makes the guilt stronger. Even more so when I read his text.

> Our dinner got canceled today. Want to get together and play some cards?

I should say yes and cancel with Jenna. This should be my sign, but I'm already too invested to have her here in my house again. I have to be the worst friend there ever was.

> I can't tonight. I have got some weekend plans, but would love to next week.

No worries, man. Hope your 'weekend plans' are blond and give you the ride of your life.

I cringe. If he only knew he was talking about his daughter, this conversation would go an entirely different way. But it is best to let him think what he wants.

> Of course. Tell you all about it later.

Have fun!

I start setting the table and even pull out a candle for the center to make it more romantic. Even if we will be going slowly, like a snail's pace slow, I want to make sure she knows I'm trying.

Just as I finish setting the table, there is a knock on the door. My nerves kick in and my body goes into full force when I see what Jenna is wearing.

She looks comfortable with her hair up, but her outfit shows off plenty of skin and her curvy body. I know those shorts. Fuck, they will be the death of me. Every time she moves, you can see more and more of her perfect ass. What I wouldn't give to find out if she has underwear on or not.

"Jenna," I smile, stepping aside to let her in.

"Here, let me set your bag by the stairs," I say, taking the duffle bag from her.

"Follow me," I lead her to the kitchen.

"Well, this is nice." She smiles and moves the candle to the side. "Dinner for two?"

Her tone is playful and immediately puts me at ease. "Yeah, I wanted to do something special for you," I reply with a shrug.

"It looks great. I'm sure it will be delicious," she says, walking around the kitchen and taking it all in.

"Want to join me out back? Thought I'd grill some steaks."

I love how her eyes light up. I know she loves good steak. You can't move to cattle country here in Texas and not learn to appreciate one. She also knows I only eat beef that I raise.

"Sure," she says.

For a moment I think of offering her a glass of wine but stop myself. I want to be fully alert to anything that might happen tonight. So instead I reach into my fridge and grab the steaks and give her a Dr. Pepper, her favorite.

When I hand the can of soda to her, she smiles, taking it from me and following me to the back porch.

Stepping outside, I take a deep breath. The smell of freshly cut grass and the sizzling of the grill fill my lungs. Jenna takes a seat at the table while I brush the steaks with some seasoning and oil. Even though I try to focus on the task at hand, I can't help sneaking glances at Jenna. The way the sunlight hits her just right, making her skin glow, is captivating. Trying to clear my thoughts, I shake my head, reminding myself of the reasons I shouldn't pursue her.

"You sure know how to charm a girl," she giggles, taking a sip of her soda.

"Well, it's only natural for a Texan like me," I smirk, setting the steaks on the grill.

As I cook the steaks, I try to keep the conversation going, but I'm suddenly unsure of how far I want to take this.

"So, how was your day?" I ask, keeping the conversation light and easy.

"It was good," Jenna replies, taking a sip of her soda. "Just working on my tan until some growly protective guy insisted I put on a towel." Even though she says it seriously, there is a playful glint in her eyes as she walks up beside me.

I chuckle, feeling relieved that she really doesn't seem to mind my protectiveness. "You know how the sun can be dangerous. I'm just looking out for you."

"I know, and I appreciate it," she smiles and reaches across the table to take my hand.

Immediately, I freeze, feeling a jolt of electricity run through my body as our skin touches. I can't deny the chemistry between us, but I know I can't act on it. Pulling my hand back, I clear my throat.

"Good," I say with a smile, flipping the steaks on the grill. "I've just been working on the farm all day."

Jenna nods, taking the change of topic easily, while her eyes glance around the backyard. "This is a really nice place you have here," she says, admiring the view.

"Thanks," I reply, feeling a sudden pang of sadness. "It's just me, though. It gets pretty lonely out here sometimes."

Jenna gives me a sympathetic smile. "I can imagine," she says softly, her eyes searching mine.

I quickly look away, afraid to let her see the desire in my eyes. Taking the steaks off the grill, I plate them. "Come on, let's head in and eat."

Once inside, I busy myself with the potatoes and she grabs us some water to drink. I'm careful to keep my distance. Though I can feel her eyes on me, I don't look up. My only hope is that maybe she won't notice the way my heart is beating out of my chest.

Thankfully, our dinner conversation stays on easy topics. She tells me about her book, and like always, fills me in on town gossip she hears at the diner. That seems to be our safe space.

Once dinner is over, we go out to the porch. We sit for a while and enjoy the night sky. Her hand is so close to mine and it's calling to me. I feel as if I need that connection more than my next breath. I don't think, I just do. I reach for her hand, and she puts it in mine.

With our hands intertwined, my mind is churning with all the things I want to share with her. But at the same time, knowing I shouldn't. This small touch of skin on skin reminds me of what we did on the dock, and it becomes almost too much to ignore.

Jenna, as always, picks up on it.

"You are still fighting this, aren't you?" She asks her eyes laser focused on me.

I sit in silence before I let out a deep breath and nod.

"Yes, I am," I say finally. "I think that it's just best for both of us if I do."

She looks at me for a long time before she nods and gives my hand a gentle squeeze.

"Then I should tell you I have no plans on giving up on us."

"Jenna, your dad is my best friend..."

"Yep, we have covered this, and he would want us both to be happy. Try again," she says with a smirk, shutting down my argument before I really even get a chance to argue.

"You are way too young for me." I know that is what people around town will think.

"I'm twenty-three. I'm an adult, I can vote, I can drink, I can go off to war. It's only a fifteen-year difference."

I can't deny her words. She is right. She is an adult. And I was a grown man who didn't want to accept the fact that I was falling for a woman who was fifteen years younger than me.

"Do you have an answer for everything?" I sigh, running out of steam to keep fighting her tonight.

She sits up and rests her elbow on the armrest of my hair. Then she sets her head in her hand, and smiling sexily, she says, "Yep."

There is that playful side that is always drawing me to her. Like right now with her so close and in my space. I'm pulled closer to her like a magnet. I can smell her perfume and feel her breath on my face. Our eyes lock, and when she rests her hand on my arm, all my reasons why we shouldn't do this go out the window.

As I lean in closer to Jenna, my heart beating faster and faster, I know that I am about to do something that could change our relationship forever. But in this moment, I can't bring myself to care. I want her more than anything in the world.

Without another word, I close the distance between us and press my lips to hers. The feeling of her soft, full lips is incredible, and I moan with pleasure as I get a taste of that coconut lips gloss once again.

She responds eagerly, her arms wrapping around my neck as we deepen the kiss. The passion between us is undeniable. How can something that feels like this be wrong?

We break away breathlessly, smiling at one another.

"I think we both know this wasn't a mistake," she whispers softly, her voice packed with emotion.

I nod, running my thumb along her jawline. "No, it wasn't. I want to give us a chance. If you can go slow and bear with me as my head battles my heart, I think we can do this."

"I can do that," she whispers.

"Okay, for now, this is just between us," I say. "We won't need to tell anyone, as we are figuring this all out."

"I've been talking to Sky and Jenna, but I know they won't say anything," she says.

From what I've observed, I know that both the girls will keep quiet. So for now, we can take this one step at a time. I know she needs friends to talk to and I can't deny her that outlet. With a smile on my face, I lean in to give her another kiss.

We sit and watch the sunset and the conversation flows easily, like it always does. When the stars begin to fill the sky, Jenna starts yawning.

"Why are you so tired?" I ask concerned.

"I haven't been sleeping well since the other night."

She doesn't have to say since the night I let her walk away, but I know that is what she means.

"Well, let's get you to bed and get some sleep. We have an early day tomorrow."

When she nods, we go inside. Then, grabbing her bag, I take her to the guest room and set it down.

While she begins to get settled in, I stand in the doorframe watching her, feeling like a lovesick teenager all over again. But as much as I want to stay with her and spend the rest of the night talking, I know it wouldn't be wise.

"I'll be right down the hall if you need me." I place a kiss on the top of her head before going back downstairs to make sure everything is closed and locked up.

Tonight, I have something worth protecting in the house and I'm not taking any chances.

When I go upstairs and pass by her room, the door is cracked open, and her light is still on. Peeking in, I find her pulling the blankets back on the bed. She is in tiny cotton shorts and as she stretches to move the blankets, the shorts ride up and I can see a large part of the bottom of her curvy ass. I have to ball my fists at my side to keep from trying to grab her.

Watching her get into bed, I get the first look at the tank top she has on. The one that is so thin I can tell she doesn't have on a bra because I can see the outline of her nipples.

Without waiting another minute, I bolt to my room, closing the door behind me. I want nothing more than to go in and run my hands all over her. But if I'm going to do this, I'm going to do it right.

That means taking it slow.

Chapter 10
JENNA

Last night I slept better in Josh's house than I have in days. I thought having him down the hall would make it hard to sleep, but it was knowing that he was so close I felt comfortable and safe. As soon as my head hit the pillow, I was out.

After sleeping so late, I was surprised when I made my way downstairs for the day. I hadn't been expecting to find Josh still in the kitchen reading and with a huge breakfast for me.

Smiling at the sight in front of me, I walk into the kitchen.

"Morning," I say, my voice still groggy from a night of deep sleep.

"Good morning, beautiful," Josh says, looking up from his book. "I hope you slept well."

I freeze standing by my chair and look at him. I'm shocked that he's calling me beautiful. Even more so, that he's admitting his feelings for me.

"I did," I reply, as I take a seat across from him. "And it smells like you've been busy in here."

"I wanted to make you something special," Josh says, pushing a plate of food towards me. "We have a big day ahead of us, and I want you to have plenty to eat."

"You should have woken me up. I don't remember the last time I slept this late." I dig into the food as Josh gets me some coffee.

As I eat, it's obvious how Josh's gaze lingers on me. It's as if he's studying me, trying to memorize every detail. I can feel my cheeks flush under his intense scrutiny, but I also can't deny the fluttering feeling in my stomach.

"So, what's the plan for today?" I ask, trying to distract myself from my thoughts.

"I got a new horse that I want to work with. I was hoping you would help me with that."

"Sure, what can I do to help?"

"She seems a little stand offish around me and the ranch hands. I'm wondering if a woman's touch might be what she needs."

As we get ready to head out to the stables, Josh grabs my hand and gives it a gentle squeeze. I look up at him and see the intensity in his eyes, and I know that something is different between us today.

While we make our way to the stables, my heart is racing. I can feel the heat of Josh's hand in mine, and I wonder if he's feeling the same intense emotions that I am.

I like this new side of him where he's more affectionate and not fighting us a couple. If this is how the day is starting, I can't wait to see what the rest of the weekend holds.

When we reach the stables, I can sense the nervous energy emanating from Josh. He's a skilled horseman, but it's clear that this new horse has him stumped.

"What's her name?" I ask.

"Good Golly Miss Dolly, but I just call her Dolly."

"I think it fits her." Walking over to the mare, I hold out my hand for her to sniff. She snorts and takes a step back. "It's okay, girl," I say softly. "I'm not going to hurt you." Slowly, I approach her and talk to her in a soothing tone. Gradually, she starts to calm down and I can feel her tension ease.

When I turn around, I see Josh watching me with a look of admiration in his eyes. "You're amazing," he says, his voice husky with emotion.

I feel a warm flush spread through my body at his words. It's been a long time since anyone has made me feel special like this.

Reaching out to Dolly, I'm thrilled she lets me pet her and stroke her mane. The horse relaxes under my touch, and soon I'm able to lead her out of the stall.

Josh looks at me in surprise as I bring the horse out. "You're a natural," he says, beaming with pride.

"Thanks," I reply, smiling back at him. "I just have a way with animals, I guess."

Then I walk her out to the round pen and begin working with her. The entire time Josh is leaning on the fence watching every move I make. His cowboy hat shades his eyes, but I get a great view of his tight jeans on that perfect ass of his.

As I work with the horse, I can feel the tension between Josh and me growing. There's an undeniable attraction between us, and I can't ignore it. Every time I look over at him, I catch him staring at me. Then he'll give me an easygoing smile.

After working with Dolly a while, she starts nuzzling me and even allows me to saddle her and ride her around the pen. In fact, she appears to absolutely love it.

"Good girl," I say before turning to Josh. "What's next?" I walk over to where he is still leaning against the fence.

"How about we take her for a ride around the ranch? I want to show you a few of my favorite spots and she seems eager to go for a ride."

"Sounds good. Go saddle up, cowboy," I wink at him, keeping things playful. But he reaches through the fence and pulls me to him for a kiss. His lips are warm and soft as they meet mine, and I feel that jolt of electricity which runs throughout my body. Wrapping my arms around his neck, I deepen the kiss and I lose myself in the heat of the moment.

The damn fence is stopping me from getting any closer. When he pulls back, looking into my eyes with such intensity,

I'm almost speechless. He places a soft kiss on my forehead, then turns and heads to the barn to get his horse ready.

As I watch Josh walk away in that pair of tight jeans, a thrill of sexual excitement courses through me. There's something about him that draws me in, and I know that I don't want to resist his cowboy charm.

I wait, petting Dolly until Josh gets his horse saddled and comes out of the barn ready to go

"What do you think? Ready to go for a ride, Dolly?" I ask her and she swings her head up and down like she is trying to say yes.

Once I mount Dolly, I turn to Josh. "Lead the way, Cowboy."

We start off at a slow pace, enjoying the beautiful view of the ranch. The sun is shining down on us, and a gentle breeze is blowing. It's the perfect day for a ride, and I feel a sense of freedom that I haven't felt in a long time.

As we ride, Josh points out different spots on the ranch that he loves. I soak it all in, feeling grateful to have this moment with him.

We break through some trees, and in front of us is a large open field.

"Dolly, let's see what you can do," I say, kicking my heels to her side.

She takes off running through the field. The wind whips through my hair, and the thrill of freedom runs through my veins.

Dolly is loving having her freedom to run. She doesn't miss a beat when we come to a tree that has fallen in her path. She jumps it like she has been doing it all her life and my face hurts from smiling so hard.

Josh gallops after me, and we come to a stop at the tree line.

"That was amazing," he says, a wide grin spreading over his face.

"I don't remember the last time I felt so free." I turn Dolly toward the creek. "They can drink from the creek, right?" I check, not knowing the property.

"Yep, that's the same creek I get the water for the house from," Josh says.

"You never told me she was an event horse," I say as the horses drink some water and cool off.

"I didn't know, but with a name like hers, I should have guessed. I got her from a widow a few towns over. Her husband had died, and she was passing the land to her kids who didn't want all the horses. She didn't know much about them."

"I'd look her up. I bet she has participated in some events."

"The way you two rode together is like you have been doing it for years. I think she was meant to be your horse," he says.

He walks over to me with a mischievous glint in his eyes. Suddenly, he pulls me close to him, his arms wrapping around my waist.

"Are you serious?" I ask, trying not to get my hopes up.

"Of course. You two ride together so well. Plus, it means you will be over here more, so I think it's a win."

I feel a shiver run down my spine when Josh's lips brush against my neck. My heart is pounding in my chest as I wrap my arms around his neck.

"Thank you," I whisper, nuzzling my face into the crook of his neck.

"Anytime, darlin'," he replies with a devilish grin.

I laugh and untangle myself from him, taking a step back. "I guess that means I'll be over here more. Gotta keep Dolly in shape and all that."

Josh smiles and takes my hand, leading me back to the horses. He helps me mount Dolly again and takes the reins of his horse. We start off slowly, walking side by side, our hands intertwined.

We spend the rest of the afternoon riding around the ranch, talking, laughing, and admiring the beautiful scenery. The sun is starting to set by the time we make it back to the barn, and I'm sad that our day together has come to an end. I turn to Josh and give him a smile. "Thank you for today. It was amazing."

Josh returns the smile and kisses me softly on the forehead. "It's not over yet," he says before lifting me off Dolly and into his arms. He holds me for a moment, our eyes locked before setting me down.

After we brush the horses down, get them food and water, and back in their stalls, Josh takes my hand and leads me to the house. When we reach the house, Josh opens the door for me, gesturing for me to go in first.

"I know you like BLT's, and I made extra bacon for breakfast. How does that sound for dinner?" he asks as we enter the kitchen.

"It sounds perfect. But you know what I'm thinking we should do tomorrow?"

"What's that?" he asks as he taking out the stuff for dinner.

"We should have our first date. Not out in public, just something here on the ranch. But is has to be an actual date."

Josh smiles and comes over to me, taking my hand in his. "I like the sound of that." Then he pulls me in for a hug.

Things are moving forward, and he seems much more relaxed here in our bubble. The problem is the bubble pops at the end of the weekend.

Then what?

Chapter 11
JOSH

J enna is right, and I definitely owe her a date. A real date where she can get dressed up, and I plan a special night for us.

So that's what we are doing today. I stayed up last night planning, and I think I have the perfect evening planned that will wow her, but still give us our privacy as we test this all out.

Today, she has been working with Dolly while I'm inside watching her from the kitchen window as I get things prepared for our date.

When she finally came to get ready, she had this glow about her. Whether it's from working with the horse or our plans for tonight, I'm not sure.

In order for Jenna to have the upstairs to herself, I got ready downstairs. Right now I'm waiting in the living room for her, going over all the plans in my head.

I almost swallowed my tongue when she stepped down the stairs. She has on a sold black romper with shorts and a black sheer maxi dress over it that has a slit up to her hip. In addition, she has on her favorite cowboy boots, which she told me before she never gets very many opportunities to wear. The turquoise jewelry she's wearing perfectly completes the outfit. Altogether, Jenna looks gorgeous and I swear I've never seen anything so beautiful in my life.

"You look stunning," I tell her, not knowing what else to say.

She blushes, a soft smile tugging at the corner of her lips. "Thank you, Josh. You look very handsome yourself."

I'm in dark jeans, a button-down shirt, cowboy boots, and a cowboy hat. It's pretty much my go-to outfit. Church clothes, my momma used to call it.

Taking her hand, I lead her out front to the ranch truck, where I have everything packed. Then, helping her in, I get her settled before closing the door. As I walk around to the driver's side, my eyes are once again caught by her beauty. She has a certain aura around her that radiates warmth and kindness.

Getting into the driver's seat, I start the engine and the sound of the truck's roar fills the air. Glancing over at Jenna, I notice she's looking at me with a curious expression.

"What's up?" I ask, a small smirk playing on my lips.

"Where are we going?" she asks, a hint of excitement lacing her words.

"It's a surprise," I reply, not wanting to give anything away just yet.

I take the road that goes behind the house and past the barn toward the back pastures. The sun will be setting soon, and we will get to watch the night sky put on a beautiful show.

When we reach the field that I had in mind, I park the truck and turn to Jenna. "Wait here. Let me get set up."

She nods, and I leave the truck running. As I work on setting up the truck bed for our cozy, romantic evening, my eyes keep finding their way back to Jenna.

She's sitting patiently in the passenger seat, watching me with her beautiful amber eyes, as if she's trying to make sense of my actions. I place a soft blanket on the truck bed floor, a couple of cushions, and the cooler with our meal. Finally, I set a few candles around that will help keep the bugs away and light them.

When I'm done, I walk over to the passenger side, open the car door for her, and hold out my hand.

"Ready?" I ask.

Jenna looks at me with a wide smile as she takes my hand. "Yes, I'm ready," she says, her eyes sparkling with excitement.

She looks around, taking in the serenity of the pasture as the sun sets in the distance, casting a warm orange glow across the landscape. I can feel her hand trembling slightly and give her a reassuring smile.

"This is beautiful," she whispers, her eyes sparkling with wonder.

Leading her over to the truck bed, I help her up and settle her onto the cushions. She looks around, taking in the cozy setup I've created. Soft blankets are draped over the side of the truck bed, and the flickering candles cast a warm, gleaming luminosity across everything.

"You did all of this for me?" she asks, her voice soft with emotion.

I nod, taking a seat next to her. "I wanted to make tonight special," I say, my gaze locked onto hers.

All this time I've been pushing her away. Now we are going to take this next step. I figure I owe it to her to prove I'm all in. The smile on her lips draws me to her like a moth to a flame. We haven't even opened the cooler, but I don't want to wait another minute before I kiss her conveying how I feel.

Her soft lips feel like heaven, and passion overtakes me as I deepen the kiss, pulling her closer to me. She responds eagerly, her hands running over my shoulders as she matches my intensity.

When we finally break apart, both of us slightly breathless, I look into her eyes. How did I fight this for so long? I have no idea, but I don't think I can fight it any longer.

"Hungry?" I ask, needing to slow things down.

"Starving," she says, grinning.

I open the cooler and pull out our dinner. Fried chicken, biscuits, and all the fixings, just like my mom would make for our picnics.

"This is quite the spread," she says, looking up at me with a grin.

Trying to distract myself from the way she's making me feel, I help her plate her food and watch her take a few bites before I take a bite of my own dinner. But it's no use. The feelings are there and they're even more intense.

Over dinner, we talk easily without any awkward silences, and I'm noticing how well we fit. Conversation flows from one topic to another. We share interests, but have enough differences that we won't get bored.

We talk about everything under the sun, from our childhood memories to our dreams for the future. I can see it now. Jenna will fit in perfectly here on the ranch, and the thought of picturing her by my side in the future is comforting.

Once we finish eating, we put the food away, leaning against the truck cab with the pillows. Our conversation keeps flowing and we have a nice relaxed vibe going.

As the night wears on, the conversation turns to more serious topics. Jenna tells me about her past relationships, and I find myself getting protective of her. I share the few relationships I've had that never really amounted to anything.

"Why didn't you ever get married?" she asks.

"I never found someone I wanted to share a home with and have in my space all the time. What I want is someone I can build a life with, and I never saw that with anyone," I admit.

When I see the light in her eyes dim, I reach over and take her hand, feeling the electricity between us.

"This weekend has been wonderful, and I really like having you here. As much as this is going to sound like a line, you are the first person I have wanted in my space. I can picture you here on the ranch. Though where I'm having a hard time is understanding how your dad and everyone else fit into the picture."

We sit there for a moment, her hand in mine, taking each other in. Then, before I know what I'm doing, I'm leaning in to kiss her again. This time, I don't hold back. I want her to know exactly how I feel.

Jenna kisses me back, her hands pulling me closer. The heat between us intensifies as I push her back onto the cushions, my body pressing against hers.

I can feel her heart pounding against my chest and the heat between us. Her hands are running through my hair as our kiss sizzles, making me even hotter.

Tearing myself away from her lips, I trail kisses down her jawline to her neck, nipping lightly as I go. Jenna lets out a soft moan, her fingers tightening in my hair as I continue to kiss and nip at her delicate skin. The sound of her pleasure ignites a fire within me, and I gently slide my hand up the back of her dress, tracing circles on her lower back.

Her body trembles beneath my touch, fueling my desire even more. With exquisite attention to detail, I explore every inch of her, my hands roaming over her curves, memorizing the way she feels against me.

"Jenna," I murmur against her skin. "We shouldn't take this any further."

When I try to pull away, her grip on me tightens.

She looks up at me with a mixture of desire and frustration in her eyes. "Why not?" she whispers, her voice filled with longing.

Taking a deep breath, I try to gather my thoughts amidst the overwhelming sensations coursing through my veins. I want her, too, more than anything, but my fear of the unknown is holding me back.

Her fingers gently caress my cheek as she searches my eyes for understanding. "I know we don't regret it," she says, her voice filled with conviction.

As I meet Jenna's gaze, I pause, my heart pounding in my chest. The intensity of her stare cuts through my doubts and insecurities, leaving me raw and exposed. She understands me in ways no one else ever has, and her unwavering belief in us is both terrifying and exhilarating.

Taking a moment to gather my thoughts, I reach out and gently cup her face with my hands. "Jenna," I whisper, my voice laced with a mix of vulnerability and longing, "we both know this is more than just physical attraction. What we have is real, and it scares me because I've never felt anything like this before."

She nods, her eyes filled with understanding. "I feel it, too," she whispers. "But if we're both feeling the same way, why should we hold back? Life is too short to let fear dictate our choices."

Her words resonate deep within me, breaking down the walls that I've built around my heart for far too long.

I lean in, pressing my forehead against hers, our breaths mingling in the cool night air. "You're right," I whisper, my voice filled with a mixture of surrender and determination. "I don't want to let fear hold us back anymore."

Then I capture her lips in a passionate kiss, this time with a renewed sense of urgency. The barriers that held me back before are crumbling, replaced by an overwhelming desire to be with her, to explore this connection fully.

I slowly gather the dress she is wearing and pull it up over her head. The smile she gives me could light up this whole town, but it's only for me. She is now lying in front of me, wearing a lacy bra and underwear that matches her dress. I don't think I've ever seen anything so beautiful in my life.

"You are breathtaking," I say, not sure how to even put it into words. The light blush that I'm rewarded with makes me even harder.

She reaches up and unbuttons my shirt with trembling fingers. Her gaze never leaves mine. The sound of each button being released echoes in the still night air, heightening the anticipation that hangs between us.

Once the last button is undone, she pushes my shirt off my shoulders, her fingertips tracing a path along my skin, setting my nerves on fire as she goes. Anxious for even more, I lie down beside her and remove my belt and pants.

Immediately, her hands roam over my skin, tracing the tattoos on my arms and chest that are normally covered by the shirts I wear. I reciprocate by smoothing my hands over her skin and around her back. Then I hesitate for a pivotal moment. Right now, we could still turn back. We are in clothes that reveal as much as our bathing suits do.

But the desire rushing through my veins is too strong, overpowering any lingering doubts. I want her, all of her, and I won't resist the pull any longer.

With a surge of confidence, I reach behind her and expertly unhook her bra, letting it fall to the ground. The sight of her bare chest, her rosy nipples and plump breasts, along with her soft curves, takes my breath away. She's even more beautiful than I could have imagined.

Leaving a trail of heated kisses, I kiss my way down her neck, and nip gently along her collarbone. Her moans fill the night air, spurring me on. As my lips trail lower, I take one of her hardened nipples into my mouth, lavishing it with attention as my hand cups and squeezes her other breast.

Her fingers tangle in my hair, urging me closer. The sound of her pleasure is music to my ears, filling me with a primal need to take her to new heights of ecstasy.

I continue to worship every inch of her body, savoring the taste and feel of her skin against mine. I revel in the way she responds to my touch, the way her body arches into me, seeking more.

Slipping my hand beneath her barely there underwear, I tease her along her slick folds. She arches her back in response, a low cry escaping her lips. Spurred on, I roll my fingers over her clit and feel the surge of wetness between her legs. When her body tenses, I add a little more pressure and watch, as she beautifully explodes. The pleasure I'm giving her takes over her body.

When she finally relaxes, our eyes meet again, and something between us shifts. Suddenly, there is nothing I want more than to be inside of her. She must feel the same way because she reaches for my boxer briefs and pushes them down. My hard cock springs free, and I'm painfully aware the only thing separating me from her is a very thin piece of lace.

"I want to taste you and make you cum like that again, but I don't think I can wait to be inside you either," I say, debating my next move.

"We have plenty of time," she says with a smile as she removes her underwear, and then a thought hits me.

"I don't have a condom." I groan and sit up, backing away slightly.

"I've been on the pill for years, and it's been well over a year since I've been with anyone. I was tested right after." Words don't even form in my head.

There is just a blank space and I try to process what she said. "You are really offering... me to have you... bare?" I stumble on my words.

She nods shyly.

"Baby," I groan, moving back over her.

"I'm clean. It's been many years since I've been with someone. More years than I should admit to." I tell her as I gather her in my arms.

Thankfully, she doesn't question as she widens her legs for me to settle between them. She then wraps her long legs around me as if to hold me in place. There is no way I'm backing out now, not when everything I want is right here.

I line myself up at her entrance, and resting my weight on my arms, I cradle her head in my hands. Our eyes lock, and I slowly slide into her. The feeling of pleasure is so deep and intense, I have to force myself not to close my eyes. Though a moment later, Jenna's close, and I freeze.

"Eyes on me, sweetheart. I want to see every emotion you are feeling while I'm inside you."

Her eyes open and focus on me, and I start the slow slide into her. She is so wet and warm, and I don't think I've felt anything so good in my life. I could cum, and I'm not even all the way inside her, but I want to feel her pulse around my cock more than anything so I hold back.

Once I'm fully seated inside her, I pause and take a deep breath, trying to regain my control before sliding back out and thrusting into her again. Her moans almost do me in, and I know as much as I want to drag this out, I won't be able to.

Reaching between us, I play with her clit and change my angle as I continue thrusting into her. All the while, her eyes are still locked on me.

When I feel her body shaking beneath me, and her cries grow louder, I increase the pressure on her clit, determined to send her spiraling over the edge. Her breath comes in short gasps, and I watch with fascination as her muscles tense, her back arching even higher.

Her walls clench around me, teasing and gripping at my cock, and I involuntarily growl at the sensation. The heat between us is almost suffocating, the air thick with desire and anticipation. Every thrust brings us closer to the brink of pleasure, and I become lost in all the sensations.

Our connection intensifies as our eyes never waver from each other's gaze. Before I know it, she is falling over the edge again and cumming on my cock. Only then does she break eye contact, and the grip her pussy has on me pulls my own orgasm from me. I've never felt the kind of sensations I feel as I cum inside of her, marking her as mine in a way I hadn't thought of before.

Coming down from this high, we don't want to break the connection, so neither of us moves. I cover her, keeping her warm, and my cock softens inside of her, not ready to leave her just yet. Seeing the beautiful flush that covers her skin, and the sated smile she gives me, makes it all worthwhile.

After one more kiss, I roll us onto our sides and pull a blanket up over us.

"Just let me hold you, sweetheart," I say, and she nods into my chest.

Never again will I be able to look at a night under the stars quite the same.

Chapter 12

JENNA

"Girl, you are GLOWING!" Austin says as I walk into the diner for my shift. "Come on, spill it!"

I think my whole body turns red from the attention.

Then she hands me a cup of coffee since we have a lull and no one else is in the diner but us, the cook, and another waitress.

"It's the older guy I told you about," I say, smiling dreamily.

"Ooooohhh! Still no names?!" she asks.

"No, he agreed to give us a chance, but doesn't want people to know just yet." I sip my coffee and watch Austin's face fall.

"He wants to keep you a dirty secret?"

"Not like that, it's just... when it comes out, it will upset certain people, and we want to make sure there is something there before we spill the beans. Also, we want to break it to them in our own way."

"Well, it's fun to stay in your own little bubble, but don't let him keep you there past when you want. Then it becomes a problem."

Right then I get a hint that maybe she has experience with that. But I don't ask, instead I let it go.

"I know, but this weekend I just got him to agree to give us a chance. It's all new, and I want to take the time to make sure this is right for me as well. No point is upsetting everyone if it isn't."

"I get it. So, this weekend was good?" She shifts the conversation back to safer topics.

"Very good. We talked and decided to give it a try. He took me out on a non-public date, and then we uhhh..." My face heats just admitting it.

"Made the beast with two backs?" Austin says, and we both burst into giggles just as the bell over the door rings.

A few of the church ladies walk in and take a table in the middle of the room. They want to make sure they don't miss any gossip if anyone else walks in.

"Hello, ladies. Are you here for your after-church snacks?" I ask walking up to their table. These ladies always meet here after some church event to talk and catch each other up on whatever gossip the other might have missed.

"You know us well, Jenna. What desserts do you have today?" Mrs. Granger asks.

"Pecan bourbon pie, chocolate Coca-Cola pie, strawberry cheesecake, and lemon meringue." I list them off.

"Pecan," all four ladies say at once, and I gasp.

"Ladies, I'm shocked. You just came from church." I smile while writing write down the order.

"It's because we just came from church. We are getting the pecan pie. We really need to get a preacher in there who can make those speeches a bit livelier instead of so dull. If you all served alcohol in here, we'd have you spike our sweet tea as well," Mrs. Pearl says.

Pearl is her first name, but because she's had multiple husbands, we just call her Pearl instead of mixing up her last names.

All four of the ladies laugh, and so do I.

"Okay, well, let me go and put this in for you. Do you need or want anything else?" I ask, before stepping away.

"Y'all have any more of that strawberry jam you were selling at the July 4th festival? My husband went through a whole jar in a week, so I'd love to buy some more if you have any," Mrs. Fischer says.

"Let me check. I think we just got more in." I head back to the kitchen and prepare their sweet tea, a plate of lemon, pecan pie, and a plate of biscuits.

"I heard them ask, and yes, we have a dozen jars of the strawberry jam. My sister is working on making more, but the baby's been sick, so she has then focused on that." Austin tells me as I load up the tray to go back out.

Austin's sister, Natalie, used to work here at the diner, but once she got married and had her son, she quit. She makes things like jams and a few other canned goods to stay busy.

Her husband Jesse used to be some big city stock market guy and saved up a bunch of money. They bought a small ranch here in town, and that keeps them busy. It suits her. I've never seen her happier. We just don't see a lot of her since her son is so young.

I head back out to get the ladies their tea and food.

Once I return with the ladies' orders, I tell them, "So, Austin says we have a dozen of the strawberry jam in stock, but it will be a little while before we get anymore because Natalie's son has been sick."

I'm met with a chorus of 'oh no' and 'poor thing.'

"My David says that there's some kind of crud going around with the younger kids. Every year, it's something a little bit different. This year, it's lots of congestion, which just causes them to be cranky. I hope he gets over it soon," Mrs. Lombardi says.

Her husband is the town doctor. She is the youngest of the four ladies here, but they seemed to accept her as one of their own, probably because she has the best pipeline to gossip with the people who work with her husband at the doctor's office.

"Parker's son just got over it. He got it from school," Mrs. Pearl says.

"Did you hear that poor boy of hers is having to head back to court again because his grandparents are trying to take more visitation right from Parker? It was such a shame when that boy's father died. None of us could have ever known that his parents were like this." Mrs. Lombardi just shakes her head.

"Oh, that poor dear. What are they taking her to court for this time?" Miss Fisher asks.

"Now, instead of just the two weeks they had over summer, they want all of summer break," Mrs. Pearl says.

"I sure hope they're counter-suing for the way that they dropped that poor boy off last time. We all saw that video, basically shoving him out of the car like that." Mrs. Granger says in pure disgust.

"When they were in here just the other day, they seemed to be in good spirits. I wonder if there's any way we can help them?" I ask, wishing there was a way to do more.

"We need to find a way to get her a new lawyer. Someone that's going to help terminate those stupid, pesky grandparent rights. I don't know what they taught that woman up there in that big city, but down here in the South, we don't treat our children like that. And poor Parker has to choose between fighting for her kid and keeping her family's ranch. It's just not right," Mrs. Pearl says, and we all agree.

"Do we know any good lawyers which have experience in this type of case?"

"Let me ask around and see what I can find, but if we do find one, they're not going to be cheap," Mrs. Granger says.

"I'm willing to bet everyone in town would be more than happy to donate something toward a good lawyer for her. After all, Parker and her family have always been the first to help out whenever anyone else in town has needed it. She filled in at the doctor's office last summer when half the staff was out with the flu," Mrs. Lombardi adds.

"She sent her ranch cook here to fill in a few days when our cook had a death in the family out of town a few months back," I tell them.

Every one of the ladies has a similar story where someone in town was in need, and either she stepped in or she would lend some of her ranch resources to help.

"But you know she would never accept help, especially not if it meant collecting donations for something," Mrs. Granger says.

"So, we don't do anything too public. We ask around, we find a good lawyer, and we give the money right to him to offset whatever she would have to pay, and we'll just make sure that it's less than what she's paying now," Mrs. Pearl says.

"I'm beginning to understand more and more why you've been through so many husbands," Mrs. Lombardi jokes.

"Well, let's go back to the church and talk to the pastor. He'd be a great person to know where to start," Mrs. Fisher says, and they agree.

"Once you get the details down, let me know. Pretty much everybody in town is in here at some point throughout the week," I tell them, and Mrs. Pearl squeezes my hand.

"You are such a sweet and kind girl. How you haven't found someone yet, I don't know, but I am going to be on the lookout for you." Mrs. Granger says.

"You promised no more matchmaking," Mrs. Fisher reminds her.

"That was a few years ago. There's nothing wrong with helping out a friend," Mrs. Granger winks, and I have a feeling there's a story behind all of this, but I don't get a chance to ask as the bell chimes, letting me know someone else's entered the diner.

That's the start of our late afternoon rush, and it doesn't stop until the end of my shift. Once I'm finished, I go home to shower, change and pack a fresh bag to return to Josh's place for dinner.

"Oh Jenna, will you be joining us for dinner?" Mom asks when I walk in.

My brother is standing in the kitchen with her, and my dad is sitting at the kitchen island.

"No, I was actually going to pack a bag and go stay at Josh's house for a few nights," I tell them. Then I watch closely for their reactions.

Josh wants me at his house just as badly as I want to be there. Only he insists that I let my parents know that I'm at his place and stop telling them that I was staying over at Sky and Dash's place.

They know I've been over there after work and sometimes before work, depending upon what my shift is, so I'm waiting for their reaction.

My dad sits his phone down and looks over at me. "You've been spending an awful lot of time over there lately," all he says.

It's more of an observation than anything, but I'm ready for it. "He got in a new horse, and as it turns out, she's a little scared of men, but she took to me almost right away. So, Josh has been letting me work with her, and I've been training her. We went for a ride the other day, and I absolutely love that horse." It's the truth. I only leave out a few key details.

Asher raises an eyebrow at me, but doesn't say anything.

"That's wonderful! Tell me about the horse," Mom says.

I sit down next to my dad and tell them about Dolly and how she loves to run, but will still snuggle with me when I brush her down. I tell them how Josh is helping me work with her and how, with my job schedule, sometimes it's just easier for me to crash in his guest room than make the drive home.

All three of my brothers look at me, but not a single one says anything.

"Well, let us know when we can come out and see you with her. Maybe next week?" Mom asks.

"Yeah, I think that will work, but I'll ask Josh."

"How is the writing going?" Dad asks.

"Honestly, the ride with Dolly seems to give me time to think. During one of my outing with Dolly, I realized I backed myself into a corner, plot wise. So I've been taking my laptop on the rides, and when we stop for Dolly to drink at the creek, there is a great spot to rest. I've been going over my story and fixing it. That spot is magical," I say.

Then I go on to tell them about the story changes I've been making and promise to have a new draft for them to read soon.

"Well, you seem really happy, so I'm glad you found something that works. Just remember, Sunday dinners are nonnegotiable," Dad says sternly.

"I know, Dad. I will be here. But I need to get going. I want to work with Dolly before it gets dark."

As I'm going to my room, Asher catches up to me in the hallway.

"What is really going on at Josh's? I know you, and I know you didn't tell Mom and Dad the full story," he says.

I'm caught off guard and have to scramble to think of something to say.

"The full story is I love spending time on the ranch, and while I never considered wanting to live or work on a ranch, the idea is growing on me. I don't know if it's just a phase or if it's where I'm meant to be, but I'm not ready to bring it up to them until I know."

"All because of a horse?" Asher says, leaning against the wall and crossing his arms.

"It's the freedom I feel on the horse. I've never felt anything like it. When Dolly runs, and the air whips through my face, my mind is free. By the time we make it to the creek, I have such clarity on my book."

"And once you are done with the book?"

"I don't know, Asher. But I know you are a planner, and you like knowing what you are working toward, but I don't have all the answers right now. That used to bother me, but since I've been working with Dolly, I'm okay with it."

"I just want you happy, but I worry about you too," he says.

With the emotion in his voice, I can tell he's being sincere.

"Who knows, maybe I will be taking you guys up on the idea of building a house on the ranch, too. I'll help make sure you guys are fed, and I'll work with horses and write. But I have time to figure it out."

"Well, you are always welcome to stay with us. I will need all the help I can get keeping the other two in line." Asher smiles and pushes away from the wall before pulling me into a hug.

"I'm glad you are at least someplace safe, like with Josh, and not on some random guy's ranch. Though it wouldn't hurt you to go on a date or two." "Maybe once I finish this book," I say before heading into my room.

As I replay the conversation with Asher in my head, I get a feeling there was something he didn't ask me but wanted to, and I wonder if he isn't going to drop this so easily.

Chapter 13
Josh

I t's been a long, hard day. I'm sore from mending fences and wrangling in a herd of cattle that seem to like the neighbor's yard much better than their massive field.

To top it off, I was hoping to be back at the house much earlier than this so I could watch Jenna work with Dolly. Since Dolly is back in her stall and all tired out, I'm guessing I missed her, and my mood drops even more.

I'm just going to warm up some leftovers and go straight to bed. The sooner I can sleep this day off, the better. The walk from the barn to the back door seems to take forever. Was it always this far of a walk?

Stomping off what dirt I can on the back deck so I don't track it inside, I swing open the door. I'm assaulted with the smell of pot roast and yeasty rolls. Best of all is Jenna in a sundress dancing around the kitchen fixing dinner.

Right then, I almost drop to my knees and beg her to marry me.

After a day like today, this is what I want to come home to – Jenna. Walking right in, I go to Jenna, and wrap my arms around her. I bury my face in her neck and hold her, soaking in the citrus scent of her shampoo and the warmth of her body.

She leans back into me and doesn't say anything. It's as if she knows I just need a moment. Eventually, she turns in my arms and look up into my eyes and I'll be a goner. This right here is what I want for the rest of my life, and I know it without a shadow of a doubt.

Then Jenna wraps her arms around me, tucking her head under my chin, and holds me tight. No matter how many years go by, I know that I am hers, body and soul, as she is mine. There is nothing I wouldn't do for this woman in my arms.

More than that, I want everyone to know she's mine, but I know I need to go about it the right way.

Gently tilting her head up, I kiss those beautiful lips. I want to do so much more than just kiss her, but I keep it light before releasing her.

"Go get washed up, dinner will be ready in just a few minutes," she smiles up at me. The hard day I had earlier is forgotten, and all I can think about is what I plan to do to her tonight.

Kissing the top of her head, I take in her scent one more time before heading upstairs. I make quick work of a hot shower to wash away the dirt and sweat from the day and put on new jeans and one of the shirts I know she likes before coming back downstairs.

She is putting the last of the food on the table. So, I pull out her chair and wait for her to be seated before taking my seat.

"This looks amazing. Thank you for this." I gaze happily at the pot roast, mashed potatoes, carrots, rolls, and salad on the table in front of me. It sure as hell beats the frozen meal I had resigned myself to earlier.

Jenna smiles at me, her eyes sparkling with affection. "You deserve a home-cooked meal after a day like today," she says. Her voice is filled with warmth and love. "Dig in, cowboy."

As we eat, the taste of the savory pot roast fills my mouth, making all the exhaustion from earlier dissipate. Jenna watches me intently, her gaze filled with adoration and something more. I can feel the electricity between us, the desire building with each passing moment.

I reach across the table and take her hand in mine, my thumb gently caressing her knuckles. Just a bit of contact and connection, hoping she understands how I feel about her since I can't seem to find the words to say it.

"I don't say it enough," I begin, breaking the silence, "but I'm so grateful for you, Jenna. I really enjoy coming home to you like this. It's exactly what I needed after a day like today."

Leaning forward, I reach across the table and capture Jenna's lips in a passionate kiss. Her lips are soft and warm against mine, and I feel a surge of desire go straight to my dick.

Reluctantly, I break away, needing to catch my breath, but not wanting to let go of her hand.

"Eat up." I nod to her plate, trying to regain control because eating is now the last thing I want to do.

Jenna giggles softly, her eyes shining with mischief as she takes a bite of her mashed potatoes. "You're right," she says, her voice husky. "I guess I should fuel up for what's to come later." She winks at me, her gaze filled with promise.

The air between us crackles with anticipation as we continue to eat in comfortable silence for a moment before talking more about our day. I share the issues with the fence and the cattle. We debate the need for an electric fence, and I find she is remarkably knowledgeable on the subject.

When we are done, we both clean off the table and I watch her move around in that sundress that hugs all her curves. She goes back to the table to remove the last few items, and I can't take being so far away. I walk up behind her once again, wrapping my arms around her.

She leans back into me, her body melting against mine. I bury my face in her hair, inhaling deeply the scent of citrus and the desire that surrounds her. My hands roam over the smooth skin of her arms and down, tracing the curves of her waist and hips.

Touching her sends a jolt of electricity through my body. I turn her around to face me, capturing her lips in a searing kiss. Our mouths meld together, tongues dancing in a sensual tango as our bodies press closer.

I lift Jenna and set her on the edge of the dining room table. Her dress rides up her thighs, exposing smooth skin that begs to be kissed and caressed.

Then I trail a line of kisses along her jawline, down her neck, and across her collarbone. Jenna's breath hitches. The heat radiating off her body is searing me. Continuing my exploration, I glide my hands up her thighs to her panties and then back down her body.

Jenna grips the edge of the table, her fingers digging into the wood as a moan escapes her lips. She arches her back, offering herself to me completely, inviting me to explore every inch of her.

Not wasting a minute, I slide my hands up her thighs, pushing her dress higher until it bunches around her waist.

Then I kneel before her, my eyes locked with hers. Slowly, deliberately, I part her legs, letting her know my intent. But she doesn't stop me. The hunger in her eyes only rivals my own.

I lean in closer, my breath in time with hers, and press a tender kiss against the delicate lace of her panties. Jenna shivers beneath my touch, her fingers tangling in my hair as she pulls me closer. Her moans fill the room, only pushing me on.

Gently, I slide her panties down her legs and let them fall to the floor. I focus my attention on her, the world around us fading into a distant blur. My tongue dips between her folds, causing Jenna to gasp. I explore every inch of her, teasing and tasting her with deliberate precision. Her cries grow louder, encouraging me to continue my exploration.

Her body trembles beneath my touch, aching for release. I increase the pressure of my tongue against her sensitive clit, feeling her muscles clench as her pussy throbs. The sound of her cries fills the room, and I swear it's the sweetest thing I've ever heard.

A surge of pride and possessiveness fills me, knowing that I am the one bringing her such pleasure. I continue to tease her with my tongue, my fingers slipping inside her, adding to the overwhelming sensation. Jenna's hips buck against me, seeking more, and I gladly oblige, quickening my pace and intensifying the rhythm.

Her moans become desperate, her grip on my hair tightening as she teeters on the edge of ecstasy. I can taste her arousal, sweet and addicting, driving me to push her further. With each flick of my tongue and curl of my fingers, I bring her closer to the edge.

Jenna's breath hitches, her body tenses, and then she shatters in my arms. Her cry of pleasure fills the room as she rides the waves of her orgasm. I continue to lap at her gently, prolonging her release, until she finally collapses back onto the table, panting and relaxed.

"I could get used to having this kind of dessert every night," I say, standing up and leaning over her, placing a gentle kiss on her lips.

Jenna's chest rises and falls rapidly as she catches her breath, a radiant smile spreading across her face. "Oh, cowboy," she says, her voice laced with satisfaction. "I want you to get used to it because I'm not going anywhere."

I chuckle softly, my heart swelling with contentment as I smooth a strand of hair behind her ear. "Well, Jenna, there's plenty more where that came from," I say, my voice husky with desire. "But right now, I just want to hold you."

Scooping Jenna into my arms, I carry her up to my bedroom. Once in bed, I hold her close. Just having her in my arms is more than I ever dreamed of. The life we could have together seems so close. I just have to do the right thing and do right with both Jenna and her dad. The problem is, I've had a bad feeling for days. I'm afraid I will lose one of them in the process.

Chapter 14
JENNA

S tanding in the pen working with Dolly, my mind keeps drifting back to this last week with Josh. Ever since he decided to drop the walls between us and see where things go, things have just been nothing short of electric between us.

He treats me like I'm the most important thing in the world, and we have spent every possible moment together. The longest we are parted is when I'm at work or when I go home for Sunday dinner. Josh skipped dinner this week so we wouldn't slip and tell my family about us before we were ready.

That didn't stop Mom, Dad, and my brother from mentioning how much time I was spending at his ranch and asking about Josh. Casually, I steered the topic to myself with Dolly and all the horse training I've been learning. But truth be told, my heart skips a beat every time I think about Josh.

Now, as I continue to work with Dolly, the warmth of the Texas sun kisses my skin, and I let my mind wander to the possibilities that lie ahead for Josh and me. I try not to think about how soon we will have to tell people about us. Starting with my family.

I know we are in our own little bubble here, but I love it and don't want things to change.

Lost in my thoughts, I'm startled when Josh sneaks up behind me and wraps his strong arms around my waist. His touch sends shivers down my spine, and I turn to face him with flushed cheeks.

"Hey there, cowgirl," he says with a playful smirk. "You've been daydreaming again?"

Josh has caught me many times lost in my own head, thinking about him or my book. He doesn't make me feel bad about it, just smiles and kisses me. When I asked him about it one night, he said he's glad I feel safe enough around him to drift off like that. I hadn't thought of it that way, but he does make me feel safe.

"Well, look, there is Phantom. I haven't seen him here on the ranch in over a year," Josh says.

I look up, and sure enough, there he is, walking toward us from the side of the barn. "Maybe word got out that you have a new lady here, and he has come to check her out and do some flirting," I joke.

Phantom is the town horse. No one knows where he came from, but we all watch out for him and feed him, and he makes his way around the ranches and even down to the diner in town.

His all-black coat glistens in the sun as he walks over to the ring and pauses, watching Dolly intently.

Josh pulls me back out of their way, and Dolly stays on the other side of the pen watching Phantom. I can feel the tension in the air as Phantom and Dolly lock eyes. It's as if time stands still. I'm riveted, standing there, captivated by their interaction.

"Isn't it incredible?" Josh murmurs beside me, breaking the silence. "Phantom always seems to have this effect on the horses. He has this calming presence that they just can't resist."

I nod, my eyes never leaving the mesmerizing display before me. Phantom takes a few steps closer to Dolly, his movements graceful and deliberate. Slowly, he lowers his head, extending his velvety muzzle towards her. I hold my breath, wondering what will happen next.

To my surprise, Dolly doesn't shy away. Instead, she inches closer to Phantom. Her ears perked forward in curiosity. They stand there for what feels like an eternity, lost in their own world of mutual understanding. It's as if they're speaking a language that only they can understand.

Josh's hand finds mine, his grip tight yet comforting. "It's amazing, isn't it?" he whispers, his voice filled with awe. "Animals have a way of communicating that we humans can only dream of understanding."

We stand there with them until the spell is broken, and Phantom runs off. Dolly starts walking around the pen, and I figure

I better get back to working with her. I turn in Josh's arms to face him.

He looks at me with a tender smile, his eyes alight with tenderness. Without saying a word, he leans in and captures my lips in a gentle kiss. The world around us fades away, and all that matters in this moment is the electricity that ignites between us.

As our lips part, we both catch our breath, our foreheads resting against each other. "I'm so grateful to have you in my life," Josh whispers, his voice filled with sincerity. "You've brought a light into my world that I didn't even know was missing."

Then he leans in again, his lips brushing against mine in a gentle kiss. The moment is sweet and full of promise, but before it can deepen, we hear the sound of approaching footsteps.

We break apart, both slightly disappointed that our moment has been interrupted. Josh turns his head towards the sound of the footsteps, and a frown forms on his face. I follow his gaze and see my brothers, all three of them, walking toward us, their eyes glued to us.

There is no way they missed that kiss, and their faces clearly show their disapproval.

"I knew you weren't telling us the whole story," Asher says.

"Why don't you talk to them? I'll put up Dolly, and then they can lay into me," Josh says.

Asher glances at Josh and nods before his eyes are back on me.

"Why don't we go sit on the back porch out of the sun," I tilt my head toward the house.

As we make our way towards the house, the tension is thick in the air. I can feel my brothers' eyes burning into the back of my head, and the weight of their disapproval weighs heavily on my shoulders. When we step onto the porch, I take a seat on one of the chairs, my heart pounding in my chest.

Asher sits across from me, his arms crossed over his chest. "So, Jenna," he starts, his voice laced with a mix of curiosity and suspicion. "Care to explain what's going on between you and Josh?"

"Well... it's complicated," I begin, struggling to find the right words.

"I'll say," Finn chimes in, leaning against one of the porch posts. "You've been spending all your time with him, sneaking around like teenagers."

My cheeks burn with embarrassment as I try to form a coherent response. "It's not exactly sneaking around," I stammer, aware that my explanation isn't quite sufficient. "Josh and I... We just didn't want to rush things and put pressure on our relationship. We wanted to take the time to get to know each other before making it public."

Asher raises an eyebrow, his gaze piercing through me. "And how long exactly do you plan on keeping this a secret? Eventually, people are going to find out."

I let out a heavy sigh, my shoulders sagging under the weight of their skepticism. "I know, Asher. And we've been discussing when the right time is to tell everyone. We just didn't want it to be rushed. We wanted to make sure what we have is solid and that it would work out before bringing it into the spotlight."

Finn leans forward, his voice softer now. "Jenna, it's not that we don't want you to be happy. We just worry that things might get... complicated if you start dating Josh."

"And when were you planning on telling us about this?" Zach interjects, his tone laced with frustration. "We're your family, Jenna. We should have known."

"You guys were the reason we wanted to make sure this was real before we told people. Josh is a big part of all our lives," I reply, my voice gaining strength. "We didn't want to rush into anything until we were sure about our feelings."

Asher uncrosses his arms and leans forward, his gaze piercing into mine. "And are you sure now?"

"I am, but I don't know how he feels. We haven't talked about it."

"Sweetheart, I am sure of us as well," Josh says, walking up behind me and sitting next to me. He takes my hand, making my heart race. This is something we will talk about later, but that sentence means everything.

"This isn't something we went into lightly. We both fought it for a while, me especially," Josh says.

"Is he the older guy you asked us about that day we looked at the ranch?" Asher asks, and Josh looks at me, raising an eyebrow.

"Yeah, he was. I was still on the fence then. Not about my feelings, but about taking the risk." Then I turn to Josh to explain. "I had asked them what they thought about me dating an older guy. They didn't have any objections then when it was just some guy."

While I appreciate my brothers' concern, I can't let their doubts cloud my own judgment. "I understand your worries, guys," I say, meeting their gaze with determination. "But Josh is not like the other men I've been with. He's different. He's shown me nothing but care and respect, and I believe in him."

Asher sighs, running a hand through his hair. "Look, Jenna, we just want what's best for you. We don't want to see you get caught up in something that might end badly."

"I appreciate that," I reply softly. "But sometimes, you have to take risks in life. And right now, Josh is a risk worth taking."

Finn leans back against the porch post again, his expression thoughtful. "Okay," he says finally. "We'll trust your judgment on this one. But promise us you'll be careful."

Zach nods in agreement, his gaze more sympathetic now. "We're not saying you shouldn't be with Josh. We just want you to be prepared for what might come."

I take a deep breath, feeling a mixture of relief and apprehension. My brothers may not fully understand my connection with Josh, but their support means everything to me. "Thank you," I say sincerely.

Josh's grip tightens around my hand, his eyes filled with gratitude. "I appreciate you giving us a chance, guys," he says, gratefully. "I know it might not be easy, but I truly care about Jenna. And I want nothing more than to make her happy. Can I ask that you say nothing to your parents? I feel like I need to tell them about this myself in person."

My brothers look around at each other, but finally, they all nod, glancing back at Josh.

"So long as you don't tell them we knew. They won't be too happy if they find out we knew and didn't tell them," Asher says.

"Deal," Josh says.

Asher nods, a hint of a smile tugging at the corner of his lips. "Alright then," he says. "We'll trust you, Josh. Just as long as you treat our sister right." The tension in the air begins to dissolve, replaced by a sense of cautious acceptance.

Josh stands and shakes hands with each of my brothers, and then they turn to me and each gives me a hug.

Finn claps Josh on the shoulder. "It's going to take some getting used to, but if Jenna is happy, then we're happy too."

Zach gives me a tight squeeze. "Just remember, sis, we've got your back no matter what."

"You guys will stay for dinner, right? I've got some good steaks calling your name," Josh says.

"Your beef, I presume?" Finn asks.

"Don't serve anyone else's on the ranch," Josh smirks.

"Then there is no way we will say no," Zach says.

"Besides, I'm pretty sure we all have some questions," Asher says as we follow Josh into the house.

This will either be a great dinner or an extremely awkward one.

Chapter 15
JOSH

As we are getting dinner going, Jenna's brothers are constantly watching over us and our every move. Jenna and I work well together in the kitchen, and I try to ignore their attention and concentrate on her. Focusing on her calms me and soothes the need to make sure she is okay.

Little things like helping her get the salad bowl from the top shelf or handing her a stirring spoon. But their watchful eyes never leave us. I can practically feel the tension in the air as we prepare the meal. It's clear that Jenna's brothers are still skeptical of our relationship, and I can't blame them. After all, I am the older guy who swept their little sister off her feet.

Asher talks about things going on at the ranch where he is working, Finn about his next string of rodeos he's signed up for, and Zach talks about all the odd jobs he takes on. The conversation flows even if everyone is on edge.

Our hands brush briefly, sending a jolt of electricity through my body. Jenna's eyes meet mine, and I can see the same desire reflected in them. It's as if the tension between us has amplified, fueled by her brothers' presence.

"I think we should eat outside," Jenna says. "As the sun sets, it cools off, and I really like watching the colors fill the sky out here."

"That works. What can we do to help?" Asher says.

"Go get the table cleaned off and chairs too, please." Jenna hands him a wet towel to wipe everything down and he heads out.

Jenna gathers plates and silverware, and then turns to Finn.

"Finn, take these out and set the table, please?" she asks, and I don't miss the look he gives Zach.

It's a look that says don't let them out of your sight. As if we need to be chaperoned.

Jenna and I quickly finish up the final touches to the meal and gather up the prepared dishes. With Zach's help, carry them all outside. As we step onto the porch, the rich aroma of grilled steaks fills the air, making my stomach growl in anticipation. The table is set, and Asher has arranged the chairs in a circle, facing the wide-open field that stretches out behind the house.

The sun is beginning to set, casting a golden glow over the landscape. Jenna's brothers take their seats, eyeing me cautiously as I pull out a chair for Jenna and then sit beside her. The tension between us is palpable, but I refuse to let it dampen our evening.

"So, Josh," Asher begins, his voice dripping with skepticism. "What made you fall for our little sister?"

"It honestly wasn't one moment. It was a lot of little things. Watcher how passionate she was about writing and then spending time helping her plot. It was how he's get upset when she got a B instead of an A at school. How nice she is to people at the diner and how she has earned pretty much everyone's trust in town." I find myself smiling at the memories Asher's question brings to mind. "It was her kindness, her intelligence, and her unwavering support," I answer honestly. "Jenna has a heart of gold, and she brings out the best in me. It was the way she challenged me, pushed me to be a better person, and believed in me when I didn't believe in myself."

Finn raises an eyebrow, still skeptical. "And what about the age difference? Are you not worried about that?"

I take a moment to gather my thoughts before responding. "At first, I let it hold me back. I questioned whether I should pursue a relationship with Jenna because of our age difference. But age is just a number, and love knows no boundaries. Jenna and I connect on a level that goes beyond age. We have a deep understanding and respect for each other." I pause, meeting each of the brothers' gazes in turn. "I care about her more than anything, and I promise to always treat her with love and respect."

Zach clears his throat, breaking the tension in the air. "Well, actions speak louder than words."

His words hang in the air, and I understand the challenge he's presenting. It's not enough for me to simply say that I will treat Jenna with love and respect. I need to prove it through my actions. I nod, determination evident in my eyes.

"You're right, Zach," I reply, my voice steady. "Actions do speak louder than words. And I plan on showing Jenna every single day just how much she means to me."

Finn leans forward, his eyes searching mine. "And what about your intentions with our sister? Are you looking for something serious or just a fling?"

"My intentions are nothing but serious," I say firmly. "I want to build a future with Jenna."

That seems to end their line of questioning, at least for now.

As the conversation continues, I make sure to engage with Jenna's brothers, asking them questions about their own lives and interests. I want to show them that nothing really has to change between us.

"I'm going to take these dishes in and get the dessert ready," Jenna says, gathering up a stack of dishes and heading inside.

The air shifts immediately and Asher's eyes narrow.

"When exactly did you start seeing my sister differently? Was it when she was still underage and thought you hung the moon?"

Asher's question hangs in the air, heavy with accusation. I get his concern and can feel all eyes on me, waiting for my response. I take a deep breath, trying to gather my thoughts.

"I understand where you're coming from, Asher," I say, my voice calm and steady. "But the truth is, I never saw Jenna as anything more than a friend until after she returned home from college. I respect her and her boundaries, and I would never do anything to betray her trust or take advantage of her."

Finn snorts, clearly unconvinced. "So, you're telling us that you never had any romantic feelings towards Jenna when she was younger?"

"Not once. She was like a niece to me. But she wasn't the same girl after those four years away. Remember, I didn't see her, not once during that time. It's still hard to reconcile in my head she is the same girl you guys used to run around tormenting as kids."

"I guess we've all got some growing up to do," Zach says finally, breaking the silence. "And if Jenna is happy, then we should at least give you a break."

A sense of relief washes over me, knowing that they are willing to give our relationship a chance. I never wanted to come between Jenna and her family; I only wanted to prove to them that my intentions were genuine.

"Honestly, I had no intention of ever acting on my feelings, but Jenna came barreling in. You all know how stubborn she can be."

"That she is," Finn says and they all laugh as Jenna comes back out with a plate of the brownies she made last night.

I watch as Jenna sets the brownies on the table, a warm smile on her face. The tension that had filled the air moments ago seems to dissipate, replaced by a sense of acceptance and understanding. It's a small victory, but it feels like progress.

Jenna takes her seat next to me, her hand finding mine under the table. I give it a reassuring squeeze before turning my attention back to her brothers.

The rest of the evening passes in a blur of laughter and conversation. We talk about our childhoods, sharing both funny and embarrassing stories that bring us closer together.

As they get ready to leave, things get serious again.

"We promised we wouldn't tell our mom and dad about the two of you. But you need to, and soon," Finn says.

Jenna and I exchange a glance, realizing the weight of Finn's words. He's right. We can't keep our relationship a secret forever. It's time to face the music and tell her parents.

No matter how I spin it. Telling my best friend that I'm dating his daughter will not go over very well at all.

Chapter 16
JENNA

We stand on the front porch watching my brothers leave after a very successful dinner. Well, at least in my opinion.

"Thank you for having dinner with them. I think it went a long way to smoothing things over." I say once their taillight disappears down the long driveway,

"I hope so, but it's also a clear sign that we need to stop hiding this and tell your parents now before someone slips up and they find out another way," he says.

Hearing the concern in his voice, I resolve to get it out of the way as soon as possible. "Okay then, we can go together to tell them tomorrow."

"No," he says firmly, his eyes still off in the distance where my brother's car light disappeared. "This is something I need to do myself. It's not going to be pretty, and I don't think you need to be involved in that. I know your dad. He will hold all his emotions in around you, and I would rather he get them all out in the open so that we can all heal and then start to move on."

Even though I want to argue, I know that he's right. If I'm there, my parents would hold back and they need to have a real conversation.

"Do you plan to do it tomorrow?" I ask.

"I think it's best," he says, pulling me into his arms.

"Then, while you're gone, I will go and visit with Sky and Dash. Maybe they can distract me."

"That sounds like a good idea. I can text you when I'm on my way back, and you can meet me here."

Internally, I'm relieved that he wants to meet after talking with my dad. I guess part of me was worried that he'd try to push me away and get more space while we waited for my dad to come around. The last thing I want is to put us on hold until someone else is okay with it.

"Maybe we should wait until after the weekend," I say as my nerves hit me full force.

He steps back and places his arms on my shoulders, and looks me in my eyes.

"You're not my dirty little secret. Refuse to treat you like you are anymore. I made the decision that I'm going to tell your dad. After that, no more hiding from anyone."

"I like the sound of that." Smiling, I take his hand as he leads me back into the house.

"Why don't you go take a nice hot bath and let me worry about cleaning up the rest of the kitchen? I'll come join you when I'm done," he says.

That glint in his eye that tells me he has plans for me tonight. "I think that sounds perfect. Don't take too long, cowboy," I say, giving him a quick kiss before heading upstairs.

As I climb the stairs, I am already turned on at just the thought of what Josh might have in mind. Quickly, I undress, leaving a trail of clothes behind me as I make my way to the bathroom.

I turn on the water, adjusting the temperature until the water is just right. With a sigh, I sink into the tub, letting the warmth seep into my bones. The tension from the evening with my brothers melts away as I close my eyes and let my mind wander.

Lost in my thoughts, I don't hear the bathroom door creak open. It's only when I feel a pair of hands on my shoulders that I snap back to reality. Josh is behind me in the clawfoot tub and rubbing my shoulders, still fully dressed.

"That feels so good," I moan as he works out the knots in my shoulders I didn't even know I had. "Why don't you get in with me?" I reach up and place my hand over his.

After he places a kiss right under my ear, he slowly removes his clothes. I watch with hungry eyes as each article of clothing falls to the floor. His movements are deliberate and I appreciate the strength of his body, his washboard abs and that line like an arrow pointing to interesting places. As he stands before me, naked and confident, I'm filled with anticipation. There's a stirring deep within me as he eases himself into the tub, settling behind me.

I lean back against his chest. His arms wrap around me, pulling me closer as the water sloshes gently around us. The steam rises, creating an intimate atmosphere that feels both comforting and sensual.

His lips find my neck, trailing soft kisses along the sensitive skin. Each touch ignites a fire within me, causing my body to respond eagerly to his every movement. My head falls back onto his shoulder, granting him access to my exposed throat as his hands explore my curves.

With gentle strokes, he glides his hands along my sides, teasingly brushing against the swell of my breasts. His fingers continue their tantalizing journey, tracing a path along my collarbone and down to my breasts. He cups them in his hands, giving them a gentle squeeze that elicits a gasp from me. My body arches against him, seeking more of his touch.

"Jenna," he whispers against my skin, his warm breath sending shivers racing down to my core. "I love you."

Immediately, I freeze. Did I hear him right?

Turning to look at him, my heart is pounding in my chest. I can see the sincerity in his eyes, the vulnerability that he rarely allows others to witness. The words hang in the air between us, filling the quiet space of the bathroom.

Quickly, I straddle his lap and look at him in his eyes, soaking in the moment.

"I love you too," I whisper, overwhelmed by the weight of his confession. It's as if time stands still, the world outside the bathroom fading away, leaving just the two of us in this intimate moment.

Josh's expression softens, his eyes brimming with a mixture of relief and adoration. He pulls me closer, so his hard cock is nestled against my core as our lips meet in a passionate kiss. I shift my hips, and with the waters help, he slides easily inside of me to the hilt, causing us both to cry out.

Bracing myself against the edge of the tub, I let Josh take control. His strong arms wrap around me, his hands firmly holding my waist as he drives into me with purpose and passion. The water sloshes wildly around us, splashing onto the floor, and neither of us cares. In that moment, it's just us and the need for each of us to give the other as much pleasure as possible.

With each thrust, Josh hits all the right spots, sending waves of pleasure coursing through me. I cling to him, my hands roaming his sculpted chest and taut stomach, reveling in the feel of his muscles tensing beneath my touch. The intensity of our connection is overwhelming, consuming us both completely.

Josh's lips find mine again, his kisses hungry and desperate. With each thrust, he plunges deeper, hitting that sweet spot within me that sends me spiraling toward bliss. I gasp into his mouth, unable to contain the powerful pleasure that washes over me.

My nails dig into his back as my hips move in sync with his. The water sloshes around us, an erotic soundtrack to our intimate encounter. I can hear his ragged breaths mingling with my own, our panting filling the steam-filled bathroom.

"Come for me, sweetheart. Let me feel you," he says, breaking the silence as he strums my clit. It's enough that my body tenses, and a few more thrusts, and I'm screaming his name as I come harder than I think I ever have.

I barely hear him groan my name as he tenses and reaches his own climax before I collapse on top of him.

As our heartbeats begin to steady, Josh gently pulls out of me, and he holds me close, still intertwined and breathless. The water has cooled slightly, but the heat between us lingers.

Josh's eyes search mine, his expression filled with tenderness and love. He brings his hand to my cheek, his touch feather light as he brushes away a strand of damp hair from my face.

"You are the most beautiful woman I've ever known," he whispers, his voice raw with emotion. "I never want to hide our love again, Jenna. I want to shout it from the rooftops, show the world how lucky I am to have you."

Tears well up in my eyes as I gaze into his soulful eyes, over-whelmed by the depth of his love for me. In that moment, all the doubts and fears that had gnawed at me fade away, replaced by a sense of clarity and certainty.

"I want that too, Josh," I say softly, my voice filled with conviction. "I want everyone to know how much I love you."

His lips curl into a tender smile as he leans in and kisses me, a short, sweet kiss before he helps me from the tub. After drying us both off, he ushers me to the bedroom and into bed.

Tenderly and passionately, he makes love to me over and over again until we both pass out right before dawn. Something has definitely shifted between us, but in a good way. I can't wait to stop hiding and tell everyone.

To do that, though, we have to face the two people that could tear us apart.

Chapter 17
JOSH

Today is the day I'm telling my best friend that I'm in love with his daughter. A million things go through my head that I could have and should have done differently, leading up to this moment. But I'm here now, and Jenna is mine, and I couldn't be happier. I just hope I can salvage my relationship with Evan.

I'm a few blocks away from the road Evan's house is on when I round a corner, and there, standing in the middle of the road, is Phantom. He is looking out at the lake without a care in the world. Stopping, I park my truck, get out, and walk up to him.

"Hey, buddy," I say, moving toward him slowly. I want to get him away from the road in case someone comes flying up, and not paying attention, hits him.

When he looks over at me, there is something mournful in his eyes. Almost like he knows what I'm getting ready for today and even knows the outcome isn't going to be good and will be sad for me.

While I know it's a reach just going off a look from a horse, but it's what I've been feeling inside all morning.

"Phantom, we have to get you off the road," I tell him.

He nuzzles my shoulder, like he's giving me a hug.

"I'll be okay, buddy, I promise. But we need to get you off the road so you aren't injured. Do you want to go to the lake or back toward the park?" I'm referring to the park on the other side of the road a few blocks back.

It's as if he understands what I was saying because he turns and walks back toward the side of the road with the park and disappears into someone's backyard.

I shake my head and get back in the car, heading toward Evan's house. Once there, I knock on their front door, and with every second, I wait for someone to answer, my heart sinks lower and lower. Janet opens the door with a huge smile on her face.

"Josh! We didn't know you were coming over. Come in, Come in. I was thinking of making some sandwiches for lunch. You will join us, won't you?" She ushers me inside.

I follow Janet into the kitchen, still nervously pacing. "Um, sure, that sounds great," I reply, trying to sound as casual as possible.

Evan is seated at one end of the kitchen island so I take a seat at the other end, putting two bar stools between us. Not that it will help.

Janet begins preparing the sandwiches while she makes small talk. "So, how's life been treating you, Josh?"

"Good. Had some cattle break down a fence the other day, and took us all day to wrangle them back in and fix that section of fence. So, I've been riding, checking for any other weak spots."

"Sounds like quite an adventure," Janet says, not looking up from her sandwich-making. "You must really love that cowboy life."

I can't help but smile. "It's not always easy, but it's definitely fulfilling. There's something about working with the land and nature that fills a void in my soul that nothing else can."

When I turn my attention back to Evan, he seems to be deep in thought. He takes a sip of his drink and sets it down on the counter. "So," he begins, clearing his throat before he speaks. "Is that all that has been keeping you so busy lately?"

Evan's eyes meet mine, searching for answers. I'm sure he doesn't even suspect what I'm about to tell him. I take a deep breath, trying to steady my nerves.

"Evan, there's something I need to tell you," I say, my voice trembling. "Jenna and I have been... dating. I'm in love with her."

His jaw drops in disbelief, and his face instantly turns red. "What?! But she's my daughter!" he exclaims, shock clear on his face.

The silence in the room is deafening as Evan stares at me in disbelief. I watch as the emotions wash over his face, from shock to anger to incredulity. Finally, he breaks the silence.

"You're in love... with my daughter?" he repeats, his voice still shaking with incredulousness. "The little girl you used to babysit, the girl who I trusted in your care many times. Your sick bastard!" He jumps up, and I do the same.

"It's not like I ever had impure thoughts of her or even touched her when she was underage. When she came back after graduating college, it was like seeing a new person. My brain can't seem to combine her with that little girl. They are two separate people." I ramble fast, hoping to get through to him.

Evan's eyes narrow as he takes a step closer to me, his fists clenched at his sides. "How could you do this to her? To us?" he asks, his voice shaking with anger.

I take a step back, my heart pounding in my chest. "Evan, please, just hear me out," I say, my voice barely above a whisper. "I know how it sounds, but it's not like that. I never touched her inappropriately. It wasn't until she came back after college and we got to know each other as adults that I realized I had feelings for her. I never would have made a move if she hadn't come to me expressing the same feelings."

Janet freezes in the middle of slicing bread, her knife hovering in mid-air. I can see the tears welling up in her eyes. She sets the knife down and looks at me, her face a mix of shock and betrayal.

Then she turns to Evan, who is now standing rigidly, his fists clenched tight.

Evan's face flushes even deeper as he takes a step closer to me, his anger palpable. "And you think that justifies it?" he yells, his voice shaking with fury. "You use your role as an adult figure to prey on a vulnerable young girl? You think that's okay?"

That's when Zach walks downstairs. Hearing what his dad is shouting, he knows instantly what happened. But he stays behind his dad and out of sight of his mom. I can't blame him. I wouldn't get involved either.

Trying to calm the rising panic in my chest, I try to explain. "Evan, please, that's not what happened," I plead with him, taking another step back. "I never pressured her or made her feel uncomfortable. It wasn't until she made the first move that things got complicated. We fell in love, and I can't deny that."

Evan's face twists into a sneer, and his eyes narrow as he takes another step closer. "You think you're the first person to use their position of trust to manipulate a young girl?" he yells, anger radiating from every pore. "If something was going on, why didn't Jenna say something or come talk to me? We share everything."

"You and I both know it would have looked even worse if she came to you instead of me. We debated this, and she wanted to be here, but I didn't want her to see you like this. I knew this is how you would react."

Evan's face turns purple with anger, and he takes one final step towards me, but I don't move. When I glance over to see Janet's reaction to all this, I also don't see his fist coming. His fists connect with my temple, and I feel a sharp pain, my head jerking to the side. I clutch my head, wincing in pain.

"I can't believe I'm even having this conversation," Evan snarls, his eyes narrowed angrily. "You're a sick man, Josh. A twisted, sick man."

"Evan!" Janet yells, rushing toward her husband.

"Dad!" Zach says, pushing his way between Evan and me.

"Zach, get out of here. You don't know the disgusting things this man has done to your sister!" Evan yells.

"I heard the whole thing. But you always said fighting isn't how we solve anything," he says.

Then Zach turns to me. "I think it's best you leave."

"And don't you dare come back! You are dead to me!" Evans yells.

As I turn to leave, I hear Janet talking.

"Evan! Think of Jenna. If she truly loves him, this reaction is only going to alienate her!" Janet cries.

My heart breaks, and I know I won't be the reason they lose Jenna. It will take some time for them to calm down, but I'll give them all the time they need.

I text Jenna on the way out to my car.

> Heading home.

> How did it go?

> Not good. Talk when I get home.

I need the time between here and there to figure out how I'm feeling and what I want to say to her. Even though I want to be honest, the last thing I want is to hurt her, too.

As I drive home, my mind races with a million thoughts. Did I make the right decision? Should I have come clean sooner? I know Jenna and I have been through a lot together, but this is beyond anything we've faced before. How can I ever make things right?

Once I pull into the driveway, I take a deep breath, trying to calm my nerves. Parking the truck, I slowly make my way towards the house, attempting to prepare myself for what's to come. Though I know there's no way around it, I'm going to have to face the music.

The door swings open and Jenna's face lights up with a smile. But it quickly fades when she sees me.

"Oh my god he hit you?!" She takes my hand and leads me right into the kitchen.

"Hit makes it sound gentler than it actually was," I grumble and sit in the chair she points to.

"Tell me what happened. Start at the beginning." She says as she walks into the kitchen, pulling the first aid kit from the cabinet by the door. I get hurt a lot on the ranch, and since I always come in the back door, I learned early on to keep one nearby. She grabs some paper towels and a bowl of water before she comes back over to me.

When she pulls up a chair to sit next to me, I put her onto my lap. Now that she's straddling me, she takes a paper towel and starts dabbing around the area where her father hit me.

Without wasting any more time, I relate what happened. "I went in, and we talked about the ranch for a few, but I just decided to dive right in, rip off the Band-Aid, so to speak." I flinch when she hits a tender spot.

The water in the bowl is a slightly pink color. I hadn't realized I was bleeding. Next, she pulls out the antibiotic cream and gets to work.

"I told him I was in love with you," I squeeze her hips to emphasize my point." He turned a shade of red I've never seen on him before. Not even when your brothers' took his new truck for a joy ride the night he bought it and totaled it."

"Oh! That is the maddest I've ever seen him. I'm sorry he got that way with you. At the very least, I should have gone. I doubt he'd have punched you with me there."

"It's okay, sweetheart. I deserved it. Honestly, he could have hit me more than once, and I wouldn't have stopped him."

Jenna places a Band-Aid over the skin where Evan punched me and then gently cups my face.

"You don't deserve it. All you did was fall in love, and you treat me better than any guy I've dated. You are exactly what any father would want for their daughter. He will come around and see it, or he doesn't have to be part of my life. That is on him," she shrugs casually.

"I refuse to get between you and your family..."

"You think I want anything to do with whoever did this to the man I love?" she asks, brushing her finger gently over the area she just fixed up.

I open my mouth to speak but get stopped by her phone ringing. She picks it up from the table and freezes.

"It's my dad," she says in a low, shaky voice.

Chapter 18
JENNA

S eeing my dad's name on my phone, I freeze. I don't want
to answer it, and Josh seems to understand that.

"Go ahead, sweetheart. The sooner you talk, the sooner you
two can work through this."

I know this is important to him, and I know the sooner my
dad and I can fix things, the sooner he and Josh can fix things.
So, for Josh and only for Josh, I answer the phone.

"Hey, Dad," I answer like I do any other time he calls.

"So, I had a talk with your boyfriend," he spits out the word
boyfriend like it's a snake that just bit him.

"I heard." I keep my tone level and as low and void of emotion
as possible.

"He's dead to me. Taking advantage of you the way he did
and manipulating you to think you are in love with him. Come
home, and we will press charges properly." My dad goes on to
say he can't even consider the possibility that I wanted this.

The tick in Josh's jaw tells me he heard it all. If this is what
Dad is saying to me, what did he say to Josh earlier?

"Dad, what are you talking about? I approached Josh with this. I was the one who kept pushing him even when he said this was wrong. If you want to be mad at anyone, it should be me."

"Jenna, you don't mean that." He says in his stern voice, the one I know I won't like what comes next. It's the one that still makes me as scared as it did when I was growing up. But I'm not backing down.

"Yes. I do."

"This isn't right, Jenna, and I forbid it." He yells into the phone.

"You can't forbid anything. I'm an adult. You don't have to approve of my every choice, but you do have to accept it if you wish to remain in my life." I tell him standing my ground.

"I've never been more disappointed in you than I am right now. Don't come crying to me when this all blows up in your face."

When I glance at Josh, his jaw is clenched and his eyes are determined. He must have heard every word, and other than the words my dad is saying must be upsetting him, I have no idea what he is thinking.

"First of all, Dad, I'm not going to hang up, run home, and come crying to you," I say firmly. "I'm going to hang up and go tell Josh that I love him and that no matter what you say or do, we'll face this together. Because at the end of the day, you can't be in my life anymore if you can't accept the person I love. And that's fine. It's your choice. But it won't change who I am or who I choose to love. Goodbye."

I end the call, feeling a sense of relief wash over me. Until I turn to Josh and see his blank stare is still there. He gently lifts me to stand and then walks toward the back door.

"Don't follow me. I want to be alone." He says, closing the door behind him.

Standing there stunned, I watch him from the window walk toward the barn. Only once he disappears inside am I broken from the trance and decide to call Sky and Sarah to tell them what is going on and get their advice.

I know Sky is waiting on an update. While Josh talked to my dad, I was such a bundle of nerves that I called her to help me calm down.

"Dash is here. He won't admit it, but he's invested. Get Sarah on the phone. I don't think I can wait to know what happened!" Sky says, answering the phone. Once we get Sarah on the line, I lay it all out.

"Well, first thing I noticed when Josh got home was that my dad punched him, and he was bleeding."

"Oh my god! Your dad is so levelheaded it's hard to imagine him hauling off and punching anyone!" Sarah gasps.

"I know! But then Josh goes on to tell me how upset my dad got and all this as I clean up the blood on his face and fix up the cut."

"Aww, getting a little nurse action," Sky says in a suggestive voice, and Sarah laughs.

"I wish. It was right then my dad called. Josh tells me to answer it, so I do. Long story short, he told me I needed to come home and press charges, which made my stomach roll. He went on to say how wrong it is, he forbids it, and then tells me not to come home when I stick up for us. I've never heard Dad talk this way."

"Oh wow," Sarah says, and the mood becomes somber. We all had so much respect for my dad. He was always so supportive of the three of us and helped Sarah out anytime he could, since her family kind of sucked.

"What did Josh say?" Mac asks. He's Sarah's husband, and I didn't realize he was listening too. It took Mac and Sarah a bit to get together, and while Sky got to see it from the beginning, I was excited I got to watch them finally admit their feelings.

"The whole time, he had this blank stare on his face. Once I hung up with my dad, he walked to the back door, said he wanted to be alone, and then went out to the barn. That's when I called you guys." I collapse onto the couch in the living room.

"I'm sure he just needs time to process it all," Sky says.

"I think it's more he wants to figure out an easy way to end it all with me," I admit.

"I don't think so. He wouldn't have gone through all this if he wasn't serious about you," Dash adds.

I'm on the verge of tears, but I feel like I'm losing him, and there is nothing I can do.

"Listen, why don't you go talk to him and see what he says?" Mac says. "Suggest you two come down here for a few days and get away from it all. I've got a couple of guys I can send up there to cover his ranch."

As Mac is talking about us coming down to Rock Springs, I'm thinking it might be a great solution. "That's good idea, And, I'd really like to see Sarah. It's been way too long."

"I can help out over at Josh's place, too. I think it will do you both some good to get away from it all," Dash says.

"Oh yes, and you can get all the Rock Springs gossip that Sarah doesn't share, and we can do a girls' night and fill me in!" Sky says.

"Or, you can come down and join us..." I hint.

"I can't travel right now, but you girls have fun!" Sky says, but there is something in her voice that hints there is something she's not telling.

"Why can't you travel?" I ask, wanting to make sure everything is okay.

Sky sighs, "Okay, I wasn't going to say anything until all this was resolved because we need to focus on helping Jenna, but..."

"Are you okay? What's wrong?" Sarah says panic in her voice, and in the background, Dash chuckles.

"I'm fine. I'm just pregnant," she says.

The line is silent for a moment as it sinks in, and then both Sarah and I scream, "Oh My God! Congrats!"

"How far along are you?" I ask.

"Only nine weeks."

"Is everything okay? Why can't you travel?" Sarah asks.

"I had a little bleeding, and my doctor suggested I take it easy and keep my feet up until my next appointment."

"We will totally have to zoom you in on a girls' night so you can catch up with everyone!" Sarah says, and I agree.

"Okay, enough about me. Go talk to Josh and let us know what he says."

We say our goodbyes, and I hang up. Taking a deep breath, I walk to the window to go look at the barn. I don't see any sign of Josh, but taking a calming breath, I go out there.

As I approach the barn, I can feel my heart racing with anticipation and concern for Josh. Saying a little prayer, I enter the building, scanning the area for any hint of his presence. All I notice is the smell of hay and animals, but Josh is nowhere to be seen.

Walking through the barn, I call out his name softly, my voice echoing in the vast space. Hearing the sound of a faint whinny of a horse in the distance, I follow it until I find Josh in a stall, gently stroking a mare's neck.

Josh turns around, his eyes full of emotion. He looks so lost like he doesn't know where to turn or what to say. I can feel the weight of the situation pressing down on him, and I want nothing more than to help lighten the load.

"Hey," I say softly, approaching him. "Can we talk?"

He nods, still not meeting my eyes. We walk toward the back of the barn and sit on some of the hay stacked there.

Josh turns to face me, his dark eyes soft and filled with sadness. "Hey, I'm sorry," he says quietly. "I just needed some time to myself. Everything with your dad... it's just so overwhelming."

I take his hand, feeling the warmth and comfort it brings. "It's okay," I say, trying to reassure him. "We're all here for you, Josh. No one could've expected any of this."

He exhales, his shoulders relaxing slightly. "I know. I just don't know what to do. My feelings for you are so strong, but my loyalty to your dad is... well, it's a struggle."

Wrapping my arms around him, I try to give him some of my strength.

"I get it. It's not easy for me either. I never thought I'd hear my dad say the words he did to me. It is hard to believe the man on the phone really was my father.

Josh nods, and we sit in silence for a few minutes.

"Listen, Sarah and Mac invited us down to Rock Springs for a few days. Dash said he has a few guys that can cover here and said we should go. Get out of town and clear our heads."

"That sounds like a good idea, actually." He says, surprising me.

I thought I'd have to do a lot more convincing. "Okay, let's do it. We'll pack our bags and go to Rock Springs in the morning."

Josh takes a deep breath and nods.

With that, we stand up, brush off the hay, and make our way back to the house. We have a lot to discuss and plan, but for now, it feels like we're finally moving forward. It's a small step, but it's progress.

Plus, getting to see one of my best friends and her family? What could go wrong?

Chapter 19

JENNA

We are on the road and driving to Rock Springs when my phone rings. We both tense as I pull it from my purse.

"It's Asher," I say, putting it on speaker.

"Hey, Asher," I answer.

"A little bit of a heads up would have been nice, so we could have planned to be out of the house and busy for a few days. Good lord, I've never seen Dad blow up like that."

"I'm sorry, and yeah, poor Zach was home and saw it first-hand, apparently," I say.

Josh told me all the details late last night when we were lying in bed talking. Even though I felt bad Zach was there, I was grateful he kept it to himself that he knew and that he broke it up as well.

"Yep, he called and gave us a heads up. We have been hiding out here at Granger Ranch for a few days."

"Do you think there is any chance of him cooling down?" I ask.

"I don't know. According to Zach, he was even madder after he called you. I'd say give him a few days at least."

"Well, Josh and I are on our way down to Rock Springs to spend some time with Sarah and her family. We are hoping a few days away will do us both some good," I tell him.

"It's probably best. In a few days, I'll test the waters and see how he's doing and give you a call. Hopefully, things will have calmed down." Asher says before we hang up.

Josh reaches for my hand and gives it a squeeze without saying a word. Knowing my brothers are on our side makes things easier. I won't lose all my family, and I know they will support us, even if it's from the sidelines while we deal with Mom and Dad.

I don't even get a chance to turn the radio back on before Mom calls.

"I don't know if I should answer it," I say.

"Best to hear her out."

"Hello, Mom," I answer, my tone even while trying to keep any emotion out of it.

"Sweetheart. I wanted to reach out after you had a day to calm down and see things rationally."

"Rationally? No, I am rational. What isn't rational is what Dad said to me yesterday." I'm still trying to remain calm.

"Just stop and look at this from our side. A man our age we trusted with your care growing up comes to us saying you two are dating, and he's in love with you. We start wondering what kind of grooming he did and when it started."

"Are you kidding me? Grooming? You are fucking sick. There was nothing between us until recently. No talking, touching, or inappropriate looks. I took a chance with my feelings, and Josh pushed me away. If I wasn't so persistent, we wouldn't be here right now. So, if anyone is to blame, it's me. I'd appreciate it if you stop trying to suggest anything else."

"Darling, you have to see how wrong this is..."

"Mom stop. Josh is an amazing person. You know that. He's hardworking and has his life together. He treats me better than any guy I've dated. Not only does he worship the ground I walk on, we work well together, and I've never felt so loved. If that isn't what you want for your daughter, then that's your problem, not ours. Like I told Dad, either you find a way to get over this and support us, or you don't have to be part of our lives. Your choice. Now, I'm going to enjoy my day. I suggest you find a way to do the same."

With that, I end the call and take a deep breath. I look over at Josh.

"Promise me something," I say, needing to know that everything is okay between us.

"What's that?" He asks, holding my hand but never taking his eyes off the road.

"Promise me that we're in this together. I'm going to fight for you, but you have to agree that you will not give up on me. Promise me you won't give me the whole you're better off without me speech because we both know it's just bullshit."

For the first time, since this started yesterday, he smiles. A true genuine smile.

"I promise because you are mine, and I'm keeping you whatever it takes." He pulls my head up to his mouth, placing a kiss on the back of it. "You are my everything."

"Josh, I promise to fight for you as well and to never give up on us. I love you with all my heart."

"I love you too, Jenna."

As the miles pass, we found ourselves in a comfortable silence in our own little bubble.

"So, tell me about these people I'm going to be meeting. How did Sarah and Mac meet?" he asks.

I'm sure he asked probably to fill the silence and to hear me talk.

Josh fits into my life so well I forgot he hasn't met Sarah or any of her family in Rock Springs, Texas.

"Well, Sarah grew up in Walker Lake. Her and Sky are best friends, and they took me in when I started working with Sky at the diner. Her husband Mac and his family own the lake house where we watched the fireworks on the 4th of July. Sky's parents were next door, and Sarah was over there all the time. Long story short, when Sarah landed herself a stalker, Mac moved her to Rock Springs so fast all our heads spun. Ever since, she has been happy and content."

"Did they catch the stalker?" he asks.

This is where I know he won't be happy, but I also don't want secrets between us.

"Yes, it was Lee," I say, and then cringe.

"The old diner manager?" he asks, tension filling his body.

"Yes. But he never touched me like he did Sarah, and I didn't find out about that until he was gone. He was rude and lazy, but I didn't know what he was doing to Sarah until he saw Mac and slipped up. Sarah's parents were involved, and it was a big mess. But he's in Jail and it brought us Austin and Natalie, so it's a happy ending."

"I'm not going to lie. I don't like you working at the diner. While I know why you do it, I won't ever tell you that you can't. Just know if at any point you want to quit and maybe come work on the ranch some, I wouldn't mind."

That instantly fills my head with visions of us living and working together on the ranch. Spending days writing on the back porch and down by the creek. Helping with horses like Dolly.

I can see that life so easily. I feel like I just need to reach out and grab it. I want to, but there are a few things in the way.

"When all this settles down, I'd love to work on the ranch with you. The diner was a way to get out of the house, earn a bit of money, and mostly see the town. Since just about everyone visited there at some point, the diner seemed like the best place to do just that."

"Well, say the word, and I'll make it happen." He kisses the back of my hand again. "So, who all will we be meeting down there?"

I laugh. "Pretty much everyone. Mac lives on his family's ranch and helps run it along with his other siblings and their spouses. Their parents still live on the ranch too. So that is five other couples right there. Plus, all their friends. This little get together they are throwing in a few days, I'd be shocked if there were less than fifty people there."

"That's a lot of people." Josh shakes his head.

"Mac's family is one of those that have never met a stranger. If you need help, they are right there to offer it. My Sarah's a friend and Sarah is family, so they treat me like I am as well. Now you by extension. You will see."

We spend the last of the three and a half hour drive talking and enjoying the Texas scenery. The blue, red, and yellow flowers that dot the landscape and fill some of the fields really add some gorgeous color along the way.

As we pull up to the ranch, I feel a sense of nervous excitement, which doesn't last long because before I know it, Sarah is running out the door and wrapping me in a huge hug.

"Jenna! It's been too long!" She holds me tight, and we both laugh like no time has passed at all.

When she pulls back, she turns to Josh. "You must be Josh. You are pretty easy on the eyes." Sarah says just as Mac walks up.

"Hey, husband here," he says, wrapping an arm around her waist and kissing her cheek.

"Nice to meet you, Sarah. Jenna has told me a lot about you. And you to Mac," Josh says, reaching out his hand to be polite.

Sage walks up, giving me a hug. "We've heard a lot about you, too. I'm Sage, and this is my husband, Colt. Let's get you settled in your room before the overwhelming introductions happen. You will be staying here in the main house."

"While you are here, we moved back into Mac's old room, so we are close. Then we'll have time to chat or binge watch some TV without me having to go back to our cabin each night," Sarah says, linking her arm in mine.

Mac, Josh, and Colt grab the bags, following Sage and me inside and upstairs.

"You guys will stay in the large suite at this end of the hall, but I'm down at the other end. So are Colt and Sage and Megan and Hunter. Their cabin is under renovation, so they are staying at the main house, too." Sarah fills us in.

"Okay, we won't hover. Go ahead and get settled. Take a nap if you want. Dinner is downstairs at six. If you want a tour of the ranch, just come down and let us know. Colt is happy to talk shop, and Sarah can show you all the changes since the last time you were here," Sage says.

"How big is the ranch?" Josh asks.

"We have just over 700,000 acres now. We are the second largest in the state." Colt says, and the pride in the land is evident.

"Shit. I had no idea. I'd definitely love to talk shop while I'm here. Even though I'm only a few hundred acres, I'm always looking for ways to improve."

"Any time," Colt says, tipping his hat.

Before I know it, we are alone in a massive room with views over the pool and the ranch.

Josh pulls out his phone, pushing a few buttons before looking up at me with wide eyes.

"You realize their ranch is double the size of the city of Dallas?" he says with awe.

"I wouldn't be surprised. It's a huge operation. This site used to be Sage's family's land. She had adopted her now mom and dad, who had the ranch next door. Because she wanted to own her family's land, they all worked hard to make it happen. It doubled the size of the operation overnight. I think I heard they purchased some smaller neighboring ranches, too, but I'm not sure."

"Well, what do you want to do? Take a nap? Unpack? Go hang out?" He pulls me into his arms.

"Whatever you want to do," I say, and I can almost feel him roll his eyes.

"Well, I want to be where you are. I'm not tired and don't really want to hide away up here, so why don't we go down and spend time with everyone?"

"Sounds good. You can meet the guys in time for you to join Guys' Night while we have Girls' Night tonight," I say, opening the door and pulling him down the hallway.

"Wait. What now?"

Chapter 20
JENNA

One of my favorite things about visiting Rock Springs is Girls' Night. All the girls get together at the main house here where Josh and I have been staying, and the boys, AKA their husbands, take the kids, and all go to the other side of the ranch to stay at Mac's parents' house.

The guys play cards and talk about ranch stuff and shoot the shit while us girls all get to catch up and have tacos, margaritas and dessert. Plus, there is the added benefit of us having a good old-fashioned girls' talk. Many a problem has been fixed here.

When I get back to Walker Lake, I think I'm going to talk to Sky about setting one up locally. Between Sky and I, we can invite Austin and Natalie and the librarian, Candy, who just got married to her husband, North. I think getting together with the girls our age to talk about things could be a huge help. For instance, this issue of what is going on with my parents would be an item for discussion. Plus, who doesn't need more friends?

After a round of introductions from Sage, I realize I know about half the girls here and the other half I've heard in passing, but never actually met face to face. It's great to actually meet them.

"Now that we all know each other, let's grab some food and sit down in the living room. We've brought all the chairs in, and there should be plenty of seating for everyone," Sage says.

No one wastes any time making tacos and filling their plates full of food. The food is arranged on the kitchen island buffet style.

"So you got in yesterday, right?" Megan asks as she stands next to me, making her plate.

"Yes, we got in just after lunch and spent a lazy day around here with everyone," I say.

Megan wasn't there last night. She and her husband spent the evening over at his parents' house.

"Did you do anything fun today?" Lily asks.

Lily is best friends with one of Mac's sisters-in-law and has been adopted into the family along with her sister Savannah, and her husband, Ford.

"Sage and Colt took us around the ranch. Josh was in his element, having the opportunity to ask all sorts of questions and learning a few things from Colt. It was nice to see what was new and talk to Sage. Getting to help bottle feed some of the baby calves in the barn, was definitely a highlight. They are just so darn cute and small, and don't mind cuddling, making it extra fun."

"Also, the baby cows are super cute," Megan says. "We had a cow that had twins and gave birth while I was the only one on the ranch. I called Hunter over because not only is he a vet, but he's my best friend. It was that night that he kissed me for the first time, and I think it really kicked off our relationship. So, the baby calves on the ranch always hold a special place in our hearts." Megan finishes with a huge smile on her face and love clearly shining in her eyes.

I tuck that little nugget of information away because that does sound like the great start of a relationship and a great way to open a book. Later, I'll have to talk to her about it and get more details.

Once everyone has their plates piled high with food and a margarita in hand, we head into the living room where there's a large sectional couch, many chairs and seating that has been brought in. Most of them oversized, like large bean bag chairs. Sarah sits down on one side of the couch and I sit next to her. Sage sits on the other side of me.

As I eat my food, I listen to everyone talking about the latest gossip in town. Megan shares about things that she heard at The Hair Shop. We talk about how Lilly's sister Savannah is a popular musician and just got married. Savannah goes on to tell us how she's going in to record her first album with the band Highway 55's new record label.

She's really excited because they're letting her do as much or as little as she wants, so she's able to work it around the ranching schedule.

"The best part is about the time we're looking to launch, the workload will be slow on the ranch, so Ford can tour with me for just a few weeks. I'll be able to tour for the album, but it won't be a huge tour like I'm used to. A few weeks, I think, will be perfect," Savannah says.

She's thrilled about all of this, and she's found a way to make her lifestyle work and still be a ranch wife, as they lovingly call them around here."The last time I was in town, someone was rehabilitating that horse that came from the illegal rodeo. Was the horse's name Black Diamond?" I ask.

At my question, Lily's eyes light up. She and her husband, Mike, run a ranch where they take in abandoned and abused horses and rehabilitate them.

"Yes," Lily says, "It was a lot of work to get Black Diamond to trust again. Getting her healthy was easy, but getting her to trust me enough to let me work with her seemed to take forever. But thankfully, Sage was willing to help because she's a genius when it comes to horses. Now, Black Diamond is the sweetest horse that I know. She's become my horse, though she's shy around guys that she doesn't know. But she and I have this bond I don't think I've ever had with another animal in my life," Lily finishes.

"It's really amazing to see she has really come out of her shell around Lily particularly," Sage says.

"We also have Snow White who came to us pregnant. Did you hear about her?" Lily asks.

"Yes, didn't her baby get some kind of Christmas name?" I ask, trying to recall the story Sarah had told me.

"Yes, Peppermint. They are both doing really well. Peppermint has become a star. She loves to jump, and Sage has been training with her. We're going to enter her into some jumping competitions and see how she does," Lily says.

"If the competitions are nearby, I'd love to come out and show my support," I tell Sage.

"Hey, I've waited long enough to ask. Tell us about Josh," Riley giggles.She is married to Mac's brother Blaze. They were the first couple in the family to get married, and everyone jokes they were what set off the chain reaction in town.

Without a doubt, I could use some advice. So when I look at Sarah, and she nods, okay, I tell them the story of how I know Josh and how we ended up getting together. I don't leave out any details. No one interrupts me, and they let me get it all out, listening very intently.

"Wow," Sage says when I'm all done.

"I can relate a little bit to what you're going through," Ella says. "Jason is much older than me, and my parents were heavily involved in our church back home, which didn't really approve of Jason because he owned a bar here in Texas. My parents just wanted me to be happy, and they liked Jason. That's what led us all to moving out here, instead of trying to convince everyone back in Tennessee to accept Jason."

"The way you guys met might have been unconventional, but so long as he treats you right, everyone, including your parents, will see that, and hopefully, they will come around," Abby says.

She's the pastor's wife and a good friend of Sage, which means she's been brought in as part of the family as well.

"For as long as I've known Jenna, her parents have been the sweetest, most supportive people. When she told me what had happened, I couldn't believe that her dad was acting like that. It's as if he's a completely different person," Sarah says.

"You and me both. I was having a hard time believing it until I got the phone call from my dad. My brothers agree. They've never seen him this upset. I think we are all hoping with some time, he will calm down and start to rethink things," I say.

"And he very well might. I think we can all agree that we hope he does," Megan says.

I can only hope they're right. Right then my phone goes off, and I pick it up, check, and find a text from Josh.

You doing okay over there?

Yeah, it's been really good catching up with everyone. Are you having fun?

I actually am. It's been really great to hang out with them. We're just playing cards to kill time now.

We seem to be winding down. I don't think it'll be much longer.

Take all the time you need.

Josh definitely treats me right, and I just hope that's something my parents will eventually come to see.

Chapter 21
Josh

I wasn't particularly looking forward to this guys' night. I know Jenna really wanted to get together with the girls and have her girls' night, and I was perfectly happy to stay upstairs. But Mac, Colt, and the other guys would not let me.

So here I am in a house across from the ranch, playing cards and talking. A lot of it is ranch stuff. Mac and his brothers are willing to help out the other men in town who have much smaller ranches who have questions or with just about anything that they need.

This is the kind of community that I want Walker Lake to be. I know Jenna mentioned something about trying to start a girls' night with Sky. Maybe I'll talk to Dash about the days the girls get together. I know that Dash won't want to be far from Sky, and I won't want to be far from Jenna. That way, we could meet at my house, and the girls could be inside having fun, while we would be outside. Even if it's just at the barn. Then I shake my head and smile to myself. Without a doubt, this is not something I would have considered before Jenna.

"Look at you over here, all smiles. What's going on?" Colt says, sitting down next to me, drawing everyone's attention.

"I was just thinking how it would be nice to have something like this back home. The smile was because I realized I never would have thought of something like that before Jenna," I admit.

"Well, speaking of Jenna, she is one of Sarah's best friends, so that practically makes her family. All of us have heard bits and pieces of what's going on, so why don't you fill us in?" Jason says. He is Mac's oldest brother and also slightly protective, so I can't blame him for wanting to know.

The cards in front of us are long forgotten as I tell the story of how Jenna and I recently got together. How I saw her differently after college, basically everything that I told her dad. Then I tell them about the meeting with her father and what was said, even the phone calls on the way here. I share how her brothers have been completely supportive of her and how grateful I am for that. I go so far as to tell them about the promise I made her in the car on the way here.

"That's a lot. The age gap alone will be hard," Mike says.

"It can be done. Look at me and Ella," Jason says. "The age gap wasn't our biggest problem. But we did have Ella's family support. I think that your focus should be on smoothing things with her parents. Not for you, but for her. She is going to need them and, later on, even want them in her life. No matter what her feelings are now."

Isn't that what I have been battling with that I haven't wanted to think about?

"I know. She is angry now, but that won't last. She has always been close to her family, and I refuse to be the reason she loses them. I'm glad her brothers are there to support her. Though I think her mom and dad can come around with their help," I tell them.

"Well, Jenna loves to write. Will you support her on that?" Hunter asks.

"Of course I will. I told her that flat out, she could write anywhere on the ranch she wanted. Whatever she needs, I will set up. However, I did say I wasn't a fan of her working at the diner, but I understood why she does it. Though if she wants to continue, she is more than welcome to, but if she didn't want to, I'd be happy with it."

"Yeah, I don't like the idea of her working there. I know Austin is nice, but she was there when Sarah was, and why she didn't quit then I will never know." Mac says, shaking his head.

"She told me about Lee. She swears his attention was all on Sarah, and she didn't have any issues, so I have to trust her on that," I say.

"With her fighting with her parents, where does that leave her living?" Mac asks.

"Well, I won't force her into anything, but of course, I'd love for her to live with me. She also has the option of the apartment above Sky's garage. She said she will decide on this trip," I say, walking to the fridge to grab another beer.

"Listen, long story short, I love her. Whatever questions you have just know I love her, and I chose her. Whatever that means in all this. If it means I lose my best friend forever so he can fix things with Jenna, so be it. Whatever I have to do, so I don't lose her. I was fighting it, but now that I have her, I can't go back to life without her," I tell them honestly.

They are all quiet and looking around the table at each other.

"I know I, for one, can relate to that. Sage and I had a rocky start. We were worried about losing our friends and family and what the town would think because we were both adopted by Jason's parents. But when we focused on ourselves and what made us happy and less on what made everyone else happy, it worked out. Keep the people in your life that make you happy, and you don't need the rest," Colt says.

"I think there are many of us at this table who can relate to you in one way or another. We all fell hard and would do anything for our girls," Jason says.

There is a chorus of yeahs and everyone around the table agrees on that point.

"Just know you have us here if you need anything," Colt says, and again, the guys agree.

"Thanks," I say, suddenly feeling uncomfortable.

We got back to playing cards before in walks a face I don't know, not that I knew any of these guys before yesterday.

"Miles! We thought you weren't coming!" Mike says.

"Well, we ... ugh, lost track of time," Miles says as he grabs a beer and an empty chair.

"Still in that newlywed stage, huh?" Ford jokes with him.

"As are you!" he fires back, and both men have shit-eating grins on their faces.

"Miles owns a small ranch and is also a state trooper assigned to the area. He plans to retire soon and take on ranching full-time. Not long after Ford tied the knot, he also got married. They have a bit of an age gap too," Jason tells me.

Then, as he introduces me, he fills Miles in on what I'm going through with Jenna and her parents.

We play a few more hands before phones start going off, mine included.

"Looks like the girls are done, and that's our cue," Mac says, and we all head out to our trucks and over to the other side of the ranch to get our women.

It looks like they had fun with tacos, brownies, and margaritas. As the guys walk into the living room, their girls run into their arms. Seeing a group of people in relationships like this reminds me of how badly I want it, too. I step out of the crowd, and my eyes find Jenna instantly. As soon as she sees me, her eyes light up, and she is rushing toward me, just like the other couples, she goes right into my arms.

"I missed you," she says in my chest as she holds me tight.

Wrapping my arms around her, I kiss the top of her head, asking, "Did you have fun?"

"Yes, I did. It was really great catching up with everyone and putting faces to the girls I hadn't met yet, but had heard all about. I'm definitely ready to go upstairs and have some us time. Did you have fun tonight?" she asks.

"Yeah, it was nice talking to the guys about the ranch and other things. But I definitely didn't like being away from you for so long. So, I'm ready to head up whenever you are."

At my words, Jenna looks around and sees Sarah right behind her, smiling at us.

Grinning, she says, "Hey Sarah, we are going to bed. See you in the morning." Then she hugs Sarah before turning back to me.

Taking her hand, we go upstairs to our room. We take our time getting ready for bed, but once we both crawl into bed, I pull her to me. Thinking of everything the guys and I talked about tonight, one thing kept coming back to me.

"When we get back, you have to get your stuff. I'm pretty sure you don't want to stay with your parents anymore. What I'd really like is for you to move in with me. Not just until you fix things with your parents or because you need to, but because I really want you there. Move in with me and let's make my house our home. Every night, I want to come home to you. I want to hold you like this every single night."

"You mean it?" she asks slightly shocked.

"Every word. I really want you to move in with me."

"Then yes! I want that too. It's what I have wanted. But I didn't want to rush you into anything, so I was going to move into the apartment at Sky's place..." she starts rambling.

Quickly silencing her mind on the track it's gone off, I sit up and kiss her with excitement.

"I want you there. I want us." I tell her, and the smile that lights up her face is one I want to put there as often as possible.

"That is what I want, too. Right now, though, I also want you."

"What a coincidence. I want you too, more than my next breath."

Chapter 22
JENNA

As I drive into town, I try not to let my nerves get the best of me. I am going to my parents' house to get clothes and the things I need to hold me over for a while. Basically, fill up my car. My brothers are going to be there to help, thankfully. Zach is bringing some boxes, and Asher is going to try to keep my parents under control.

My brothers say my parents are still pretty mad, so we have no idea what to expect. This morning, I let them know I was coming to pick up a few things. I need to get my more clothes, including my working uniform. Also, I'd like to grab some books and my computer along with whatever else I can get in my car. Josh said I should make plans with my parents while I'm here to get the rest of my things.

So, as I turn onto my parent's road, I go over what I plan to say in my head for about the hundredth time. What I want to do is stay nice and calm, keep it short and sweet, and to the point. I'm hoping they will listen and maybe I can get through to them so we can start healing. Josh won't say it, but I know being at odds with my parents like this really bothers him. I want to fix things for him because he is giving up so much for our relationship.

When I pull into the driveway, my nerves kick into full gear. My brothers are waiting on the front porch for me, and it helps to see their friendly faces. They greet me with hugs as I step out of my car.

"Hey, guys. How have you been?" I ask, once I hug each of them.

"Just trying to keep busy. We feel it's best at this point." Zach says, and the others agree.

"Yeah, I get that." I nod.

"How was your trip to Rock Springs?" Asher asks.

"It was so good. Exactly what we needed. It was nice to be around other couples who had a rocky start but ended up working things out. Josh got to talk 'ranch shop' with the guys. With the girls, I got to vent and get some advice. We went horseback riding, and Megan had me come into the shop for a manicure and pedicure." I flash my red, white, and blue nails she did for me so they can see.

I don't know how long the nails will last working at the diner, but I know everyone will like them while they do.

"Those are fancy," Finn says.

"Yeah, she wanted to post photos up on social media to draw in clients looking for summer themes, and I was happy to be her guinea pig."

"Well, let's get this over with. Remember, we have your back. Just try to stay calm. Get in and get out," Asher says.

I follow them into the house and to the back family room, where both my mom and dad are sitting beside each other on the couch.

"Hello, Jenna," Dad says. His voice is cold and emotionless, letting me know this isn't going to be a big, happy family reunion. Not that I thought it would be.

"Hi, Mom and Dad. I wanted to let you know of my intention to move out. Today, I'm here to get my clothes and things to hold me over until an agreed-upon time. Later, I will have a few people come help me get the rest of my clothes, books, and other stuff." I tell them, as proper and as matter of act as possible. I'm not asking for permission. I am telling them what I plan to do.

"Ethan!" Mom whispers to my dad. I don't think I was meant to hear it, but I did.

"Where will you be moving to?" Dad asks. His voice is still level. I have a feeling that is about to change.

I look over at Asher, who is leaning against the wall to my right, and he realizes what he is about to say, and his eyes go wide for a moment. When I glance over at Zach and Finn, who are sitting at the kitchen island eating whatever snack Mom left out, Finn smirks and Zach shakes his head.

"Josh asked me to move in with him, and I agreed," I say, waiting for their response.

My dad clenches his jaw, and the vein on his forehead starts throbbing.

"Not that you will listen, but I don't approve of you moving in with your boyfriend," Dad spits the word boyfriend out like it's poison.

"You don't approve of me living with any boyfriend or just because it's Josh?" I ask.

When my dad doesn't reply, I have my answer.

"I feel so sad for you. You can't get past your own blinding anger to see how you are destroying everything around you. Your family and your friends are all falling apart because you are so narrow-minded," I say to him.

"Jenna. Let sleeping dogs lie," Asher says.

I take a deep breath and nod.

"We are both here when you are ready to talk. I pray that is soon and not in several decades on your deathbed when you realize how much you messed up," I say. Then, turning on my heels, I go upstairs, followed by my brothers.

"You were very calm. I'm proud of you," Asher says, giving me a hug when we reach my room.

"I feel anything but calm, so I'm glad I at least appeared that way."

"What can we help you pack?" Finn asks.

"Well, I need pretty much everything on my desk," I start.

"Got it!" Finn says, grabbing a box.

"Zach, can you pack up these two rows of books?" I point to my bookcase.

"No problem," he says, also grabbing a box.

"Want me to start on the bathroom items?" Asher asks.

"Yes, and I'll pack clothes. Once all those are in my car, I want to load up all the clothes I can. When Dad calms down, if you can get him out of the house so Josh and I can come back and get the rest, that would be great." I tell him while I pack my suitcases.

"There's a property we saw the other day. It wasn't perfect, but I could ask him to go take a look at it with me. Probably I could guilt him into it. It would buy you about three hours since it's pretty close to Amarillo," Asher says.

"That would be perfect. I won't have much after today, just books and clothes." I look around.

"I'll pack up all the books and leave the boxes in here for you. Same with the closet if you want," Finn says.

"That would be a huge help if you could do it without getting in trouble. No reason to have Mom and Dad mad at you guys, too."

As we gather everything together, we talk about how things are going with them.

THE COWBOY AND HI BEST FRIEND'S DAUGHTER   189

"Desk is done, so I will take this down to your car. I also have your computer and charger in your bag here. Want that in the car, too?" Finn asks.

"Yes, please. The computer can be in the front seat," I say as he heads out.

Both Zach and Asher take their boxes down to the car, too. Then the guys take down my suitcases and duffle bags that I'd packed. Before I know it, my car is packed, and it's time to head back down and say goodbye to my mom and dad.

"We will meet you by your car," Finn says as we go downstairs. While I go back to the family room, they go outside.

Facing my hostile looking parents, I try to keep it short before I lose my emotional control. "Well, I am going. I love you both," I say sincerely.

Neither of them says a word. I can tell Mom wants to just by the look on her face, but I also know she will support my dad, even if she doesn't agree with him. Maybe she can talk some sense into Dad, and we can end this soon.

Once I'm outside, I give each of my brothers a hug.

"I really miss Sunday dinners. How do you guys feel about coming over Friday night and having dinner with us? Start our own little tradition?" I ask.

The guys look a bit guilty, and each gives the other a look I can't quite read.

"What is it?" I ask, already annoyed.

"It's not that we don't want to. It's just..." Finn trails off.

"Friday nights are date nights." Zach finishes, and my heart sinks. Of course, they have dates and lives of their own.

"But if you can do it Thursday night, we can do that," Asher says, and just like that, I'm feeling better.

"That works. And we will be at your rodeo too, Finn. I promise we'll keep away from Mom and Dad in order to keep the peace. But I haven't missed one of your local shows yet, and I don't plan to start now." I give him a hug.

"Good, I want you there," he says.

After a few more goodbyes, and promises that they'll see me on Thursday, I'm on the road back to Josh's, back home.

Chapter 23
JOSH

I just got in early from checking on the cattle, and Jenna sent me to clean up. Today, her brothers are coming over, and I can feel the nervous energy coming off her. She wants the meal to be perfect and replace her mom's Sunday dinners. Ultimately, I think she just wants that feeling of family around.

Knowing this is important to her, I make sure to put on a good pair of jeans and a nice shirt. I also spray on some of that cologne she likes before heading back downstairs.

I find her fussing around the kitchen.

"Sweetheart, the food smells amazing," I tell her as I walk up behind her and wrap my arms around her waist.

She feels so good pressed against me. I lean in and kiss her neck, and she melts into me.

"If we had the time, I'd have you right here on the counter. A few orgasms should help relax you," I tell her as I run my hands down her sides teasing, the hem of her dress.

"Now, I will be thinking of that all night," she moans.

"Good, so will I," I say pressing my hard cock into her to let her know how much I want her.

Cupping her breasts, I'm hoping we can squeeze in a quicky when the doorbell rings.

"Dammit," I groan, wanting more time with her.

Laughing, she turns in my arms and places a kiss on my cheek.

"Tonight, we can reenact this moment. Now cool off, I'll get the door." Then she winks at me, leaving me alone in the kitchen to get myself under control.

I listen as she greets her brothers. When I see the sauce on the stove boiling away, I give it a stir as they join me in the kitchen.

"Hey," I greet them, and they settle on the kitchen island while we talk and finish up dinner prep.

It really is fun catching up with them on how ranch plans are going and Finn's upcoming rodeo. Jenna has been talking about it nonstop, and she is excited to go.

"So, I know this is short notice. But we got Mom and Dad helping us look at a place tomorrow morning. If you two can get into the house then to get your stuff, that would be great. If not, it won't be until next week," Asher says.

"Do you think we can do it?" Jenna asks, looking at me.

"I will make it happen. How much stuff do you have left? Will we need another truck?"

"Based on her books alone, yeah, another truck would be helpful," Finn says with a chuckle.

"I'll ask Dash and Jesse to come help. Better to have a few extra hands, too," I say, thinking out loud.

"Well, enough of that. Let's get the table ready. It's time to eat!" Jenna says.

Everyone chips in, sets the table, gets drinks, and brings the food to the table. It's a hot Texas day, so we are eating inside in the air conditioning. Though I will say it feels a little like Sunday dinners if you don't think about her parents not being here. The conversation flows, her brothers are telling jokes, and we are catching up on the doings during the week. There is ranch talk and talk of Jenna's book and gossip in town.

Looking around the table, I realize this woman has brought me a family. I always felt just outside of her family, but here, having dinner at our house feels different.

"I was talking to a friend of mine, and he is looking to sell his ranch. It isn't on the market yet, but I told him that you guys want to buy one and your story. He doesn't want to sell to the land developers sniffing around here. Since he wants someone to keep running it as a ranch, he's interested in meeting you boys," I tell them.

I hadn't even had a chance to tell Jenna this yet, so it's news even to her.

"What ranch is it?" Asher asks.

"Is it here in town?" Finn asks at the same time.

"Yes, it's here in town. You'd actually butt up to part of my land on the north side. It's the Silver Cattle Ranch. Willy and I are old friends." I answer their questions patiently.

"That's a beautiful ranch, but way out of our price range," Asher says, looking defeated.

"Well, let's go talk to him. It can't hurt to take a look and see what he's thinking. He said he'd make you a good deal just to stick it to the land developers who are always nosing around. And if you need a little help, I'd be willing to go in as an investor, and you buy me out at the same price I buy in when you can," I tell them.

"Why would you do that?" Zach asks.

"Because when you found out about us, you didn't turn your backs on Jenna. You supported her, and you have been a big help to your parents. I'm grateful for you supporting her, and I hope one day, maybe soon, we will be family. It's what family does." I say, but my eyes are locked on Jenna, hoping she gets my meaning.

I am in this for the long haul, and this ends with her being my wife. Right now, I want to give her time to adjust to everything going on. She's just moved in. There is all the tension with her parents, and I don't want to take that step until everything has calmed down. But I do plan on making her my wife.

Jenna's eyes go wide, and she stares back at me. Her beautiful eyes are misty with unshed tears.

Leaning close to her as I can, I give her a kiss on one cheek. "Don't cry, sweetheart. I meant it when I said I was all in."

Jenna takes my hand in hers, and takes a deep breath before turning back to her brothers, who watched the whole thing.

"What do you think? It can't hurt to go see what Willy has to say. And if it's okay, I'd like to go with you," Jenna says.

"Well, it can't hurt to go talk to him," Asher says hesitantly.

"You are always welcome, Jenna," Finn says, and the others agree.

"I will set up a time. When works for you guys?" I ask.

They all agree that any time on Monday or Tuesday works best. After they leave tonight, I make a note to call Willy to set it up.

The rest of the night goes by pretty quickly. There's lots of laughter, stories, and just talking with them makes for a good time. Once the topic switched to town gossip, Jenna really lit up because she heard the best of it at the diner. While in the kitchen, I clean up, wanting her to have this time with her brothers.

After they leave for the night, she pulls me back toward the kitchen.

"Hmm, I think we have some unfinished business this evening," she says. Then she jumps up on the kitchen counter and winks at me.

I step between her legs, causing her dress to ride up to her hips. Taking a moment to memorize every detail about her, as I always want to remember this moment. The way the light shines in her hair, the way the dress hugs her curves, and the way it feels to have her legs around my hips, is not something I want to forget.

"You are so damn beautiful," I tell her and watch her cheeks fill an attractive shade of pink. "It's true. I don't know what made you fall for an old cowboy like me, but I'm so damn grateful every day for it."

Then I kiss in a way that I hope conveys my love for her. It's soft, gentle, but urgent. She wraps her arms around my neck and tries to pull me in, but I keep it slow. Tonight, I'm in no rush. I want to show her exactly how I feel. When she tries to grind against me, I place my hand on her hips and keep her still.

"I'm not rushing tonight. We have all night, and we are just getting started. Taking it slow," I whisper against the skin of her neck as I lightly drag my lips across her delicate skin, causing it to pebble.

I love how responsive she is to me and how easily I can get her body to react to me. I'm enjoying learning about her body, like how nibbling at the spot at the base of her neck and collarbone causes her to moan every time. She is slightly ticklish on her side, right under her breasts, and a simple foot rub can make her melt and groan in ways that make me so damn hard.

"Hold on baby," I say, wrapping her legs around my waist and picking her up off the counter.

And now, I love the way she holds on to me and trusts me as I carry her upstairs to our room. It's time I reward that trust.

Chapter 24

JENNA

Today, we are touring Silver Cattle Ranch. There have been times that I've talked to Willy in the diner, and he's super sweet. I didn't know he was looking to sell it until Josh mentioned it, though.

"Jenna!" He greats me the same way he always does at the diner. "You coming to tour the ranch with your brothers today?" he asks, and then his eyes land on mine and Josh's intertwined hands.

"Oh, or you here with Josh?" He says, raising an eyebrow, but there isn't any judgment in his tone.

"A little of both," I say, not sure what Josh wants to tell him.

"Yeah, we have been dating for a while. A lot has been happening since the last time we talked. Jenna just moved in with me," Josh says with pride.

I love that he is so open about us to the people in his life. It really does make all the difference.

"Good for you, old man. Landing a sweet youngster like that is the dream," Willy says.

Then he turns to me, "If he doesn't treat you right, you let me know. I got some ranch hands that would rough him up a bit on your behalf any day, young lady."

We both laugh as my brothers pull into Willy's driveway. All three of them are piled into Asher's work truck and it's humorous seeing these big cowboys come tumbling out.

"Hey, I haven't seen you three in a while. Man, you have grown into some heartbreakers, haven't you?" Willy says as he greets them.

"They have, and they know it too. Especially Finn out there riding those damn bulls," I say.

"Well, let me show you around and then we can go in and talk. I got some of those cookies from the diner yesterday before they sold out. Even though I almost ate them all last night, I stopped in time to share them. Let's hop on the buggy here," Willy says.

The buggy is a six-seater all-utility vehicle. We all get on and off we go. He shows us the grounds, and finally ends up at the barn. In the barn's office, he has a map with the property lines and some overhead views.

"It's perfectly set up to build the two other houses right by the road," Finn says, looking at the map then at me. "There is even room for your own place if things don't work out with Josh."

Josh grunts at that, wrapping his arm around my waist, and pulling me close like he hates even the idea of me leaving.

"I'm not going anywhere," I whisper to him.

"Damn right you aren't," he says, kissing the top of my head.

My brother talks cattle with Willy. I understand most of it, but not everything they are talking about. What I do get is that Willy has slowed down his operation quite significantly because he just can't handle it all. The cows on the property are about a tenth of what the property can hold, and they would be included in the sale.

"How many head of cattle can this place hold at max capacity?" Zach asks.

"Over 218 was the most we had, and I feel like I wouldn't have wanted to go over that. We also have a few people that board their horses here from the city. You add in some horse training like I am hearing Zach here is good at and you should do very well," Willy says.

I remember them talking about horses too, so I know it's something Zach is interested in. We tour the barn, the bunkhouse for the ranch hands, and a few of the pens and outbuildings. Then we head inside and tour the house.

"This place is beautiful," I say, looking around at all the old details that you don't see much anymore.

"My grandfather built this place with the help of his two brothers. That's how the land started with three brothers, so I think it's only right three brothers' take it over," Willy says with a sad smile.

"I don't mean to push, but what about your son?" Asher asks.

"That's a valid question. He has no interest in ranching. He'd rather go out all night partying and getting tattoos. Eric always had eyes for the city and couldn't get out of there fast enough. He kept pressuring me to sell to the land developers when he saw what they were offering. He just wants the money, but it will be a cold day in hell before I let them take over the land. It means more to me to see you three taking it over and loving it as my dad and grandfather did than to get top dollar. It will upset Eric since all he seems to care about is his inheritance, but so be it," Willy says.

"What are your plans when you sell it?" Finn asks.

"Well, I met a nice lady who has retired in Sedona. I reckon I will join her and do some traveling. I wasn't able to do much while running this place, and I'd like to see a few things before I kick the bucket."

"Let's sit at the table. I know the not-so-fun part of the talk is coming," Willy says.

When we follow him to the dining room, he sets out some cookies and a pitcher of sweet tea before he grabs a folder off the counter.

"Let's be honest here. I've looked up what this place is valued at, and it's out of our price range, at least as it stands right now," Asher says.

"I figured as much. But I also did my own research and put together a few things," Willy says, sliding the folder across the table to Asher.

I can't see what is in the folder from here, but Asher's eyes go wide, and Zach and Finn crowd in around him, reading whatever it is.

"Are you serious?" Finn says. "This is less than the land itself is worth. It doesn't include the cattle and horse boarding side of it."

"My granddaddy and his brother bought this place for half its worth. They built it up, and my dad took it on and then me after. My grandad had no illusions that every generation would want to run the land. Ranching is hard work. So, I remember him telling me if I were ever to sell it, I should find someone with love for the land and make them a good deal since our family got a good deal on it."

Asher looks over at Josh. "Are you serious about backing anything we would need? With these numbers, we would only need a little and could pay it back in just a few years."

"One hundred percent serious, whatever you need," Josh says.

"Do you mind if we step outside and talk for a few minutes?" Asher asks.

"Heavens no. You boys take the time you need. I only ask you don't tell anyone I'm thinking of selling. I don't need it getting out just yet," Willy replies.

"We understand. We won't say a word," Finn says.

Then the three of them go out to the front porch to talk.

"Now, how did you two hide from the town for so long? Because I haven't heard a peep in town about you two," Willy says.

"Mostly, we haven't left the house. We just told Jenna's parents the other day," Josh says.

"And how did that go?"

"Not good," Josh says, rubbing the spot where my dad punched him.

"I would reckon not," Willy chuckles.

"I know Evan is nothing but rational. He always thinks first, but that there is his little girl. I don't think he's being rational. I think it will take him some time to come around. Just treat her the way she should be treated, and he will see that, and I think that is all it will take," Willy says wisely.

"I wish I had your confidence. My dad... well, I never saw him that way before, and I have seen him angry. The things he said. I never thought I'd hate my father, but it came really close after that phone call," I say, trying not to let the tears fall that fill my eyes.

"There is a real fine line between love and hate. If you didn't love him so much, you wouldn't feel such strong emotions over this. Don't let it go too long before talking to him. Though you might have to make the first move. It's okay to take some time to cool off and regroup, but you don't let Thanksgiving come around before you talk to him, you hear?" Willy says in that stern grandfather's voice.

All I can do is nod because the back of my throat burns, and I'm trying so hard not to cry, just thinking about heading into the holidays without my parents. If we can't work it out by then, I worry we never will, and that would break me. I can't even think what that would do to Josh or what he's trying to do to fix things. I take a deep breath and stop letting myself go down that road.

Josh seems to understand how I'm feeling because he pulls me to his side and holds me close as my brothers come back into the house. They are all wearing smiles, and I know the answer before they even speak.

"We talked, and we have some things to work out, but we'd love to buy Silver Cattle Ranch. And Josh, we would like to take you up on your offer to invest as well," Asher says excitedly.

You can see the pure joy and exhilaration on their faces. This is what they have been working toward. It's in town, they will be my neighbor, and the property is exactly what they wanted.

With Josh's help they are finally able to make their dream come true. It's a win-win.

I jump up and hug them each.

"Oh my gosh, I'm so excited for you guys, and I got to be here to see it all happen! If you guys don't let me help you decorate, I will be so mad!"

Everyone starts talking at once until a loud whistle screams through the air. We all turned to find it had come from Willy.

"How about you boys take the buggy and go do some planning? I will call up my attorney and get the paperwork started. Again, let's keep this under wraps as much as possible until the papers are signed. Also, be warned those land developers won't be too happy, so expect some grumbling from them," Willy says.

"We are going to go on home and let you guys get to planning," Josh says. "Let me know what you need, and I will be there. I echo Jenna in that I will be mad if you don't let me help any way I can."

After hugs all around, we leave for home.

My brothers will be my neighbors, and they finally get to realize their dream. Now I am living my dream, so all that is left is to get Mom and Dad on board with it all.

Easy, right?

Chapter 25
JOSH

Today, we are in Amarillo to support Finn at his rodeo. I've been to this before with the family, but today is different. This day, Jenna and I aren't holding anything back, and we're not keeping us a secret. Her brothers have seen us together, but this is our first official outing, and I know people from town will be here to support Finn, too.

Once I park my truck, I turn to Jenna.

"Are you ready to do this? Be public with us?" I ask, wanting to make sure I'm not pushing her into anything.

"Yes, I am," she says, taking my hand. "Are *you* sure about this? I'd understand if you want to keep it a secret a bit longer."

"Not only do I not want to keep you a secret, I want to tell everyone you are mine." I tighten my grip on her hand to make my point. Then I cup the back of her neck and pull her in for a kiss.

Getting out of the truck, I go around to her side, opening the door and helping her out. Then, taking her hand, we walk toward the entrance to the rodeo.

"There are my parents," she says and when I look up, they are watching us from the other parking aisle. Looks like they got here at the same time we did. Asher and Zach are with them. Finn has probably been here since daybreak, soaking everything up because he loves the attention and everything that goes with it.

We walk toward the entrance hand in hand, quietly, knowing we will run into her parents when we get there. I try to give some of my strength to her because I know this can't be easy for her.

"Hello, Mom and Dad." Jenna greats them like you would a professor you didn't like in school. She then lets go of my hand and hugs Asher and Zach with a smile lighting up her face. We stand there for a moment, her dad not even looking our way.

"Well, it was good to see you," Jenna says, and then takes my hand, and we find some seats. As we walk away, I can hear Asher talking to her parents.

"Is this really how it's going to be? You aren't even going to acknowledge your own daughter?"

"Yeah," Zach says, "Are you so stuck in your own world that you are missing how truly happy she is and how great he treats her? Would you rather she be with some asshole that beats the shit out of her?"

At Zach's words, I almost stop in my tracks.

"Don't get involved," Jenna says, tugging on my arm.

We don't get to hear the rest of the conversation as we get in line to get some food and water before taking our seats. We're close enough to the front to have a good view, but not near enough to get hit by all the dust. Best of all, our spot has a nice amount of shade.

"Good to see you two out and about." Ben sits down on the bleachers beside us. He's one of the cops from Walker Lake and a hobby rancher, at least for now.

"Yeah, we came to support Jenna's brother. She hasn't missed a single local rodeo. We weren't going to start now," I tell him.

"When I stopped in the diner for lunch, Jenna told me a little about what happened. Let me know if you need anything."

"Thank you," I say. His support means a lot. I know many people respect him, and if we have his support, then others will follow. It will just take time.

Finn is in two different events: steer wrestling, where he jumps off a horse to tie down a calf, and, of course, the big one, bull riding. That is a popular event, and they always save it for the end to get everyone to stay for the entire show. While Finn is up for the steer wrestling, Jenna is on her feet, cheering as loudly as she can. Her parents are sitting in the next section over, and when I glance that way, they are watching her, and they are watching me. Let them watch. I have nothing to hide.

Finn gets a near-perfect score, earning him first place, which in this rodeo means he's walking away with about $5,000. Nothing to laugh at.

"Hey, we have some time before the next round. Do you want to go to the restroom and walk around?"

"Yeah, I want to look at some of the booths and get a snack," she says.

"Hey, Ben. Jenna wants to walk around. Will you save our seats?" I ask.

"You got it. Just bring me back water?" He pulls out his wallet.

"Of course, and I got it," I say.

Smiling, he puts his wallet away, thanking me."

We walk the booths, which are geared toward the city people wanting to be cowboys and cowgirls for the weekend. Brand new boots and cowboy hats, marked up with rodeo prices abound, of course. There is a mechanical bull riding tent where those who want to try their hand at the sport congregate. We hit the restrooms first. It's a large row of parapets, and we run into her parents there too. We exchange a simple nod of heads, but nothing else.

While Jenna uses the restroom, I hold her purse and hat and have hand sanitizer ready for when she steps out. She walks out with a smile, then uses the sanitizer before taking her bag. I gently place her hat back on her head, and she smiles up at me like I hung the moon. Once again, I take her hand, and we walk some of the stalls, looking at everything from dreamcatchers to paintings and decor made from only horseshoes.

"A few years ago, at one of these booths, they had a shoe rack made from old horseshoes. I really loved it, but it was too bulky to get home and really, where would I have put it? If we can find something like that again, I think it would be great at your place," she says.

"Our place, sweetheart. It's our place," I tell her. No matter how long I live, I don't think I will ever forget the look in her eyes when she looks up at me. The love and emotion are clear as day on her face. Without thinking, I plant a kiss on her right there in front of everyone.

When I pull away, the smile on her face is even bigger.

"Let's get some water and go back to our seats," I say.

"I think I want to make a slushie," she says, pointing to a booth. Her wish is my command, so we head over to get her slushie and water for Ben and me before returning to our seats.

We watch a few more events, and I can't seem to keep my hands off her. Either I'm rubbing her back or holding her. She doesn't seem to mind as she melts into my side and rests her head on my shoulder. It all feels so natural, and I love taking care of her. The only downside is every time I glance up, her dad is watching us with a look on his face I can't quite figure out. I'm not sure I even want to.

After a few minutes, Jenna turns to me.

"I think I could use water. That slushie had too much sugar."

"Alright, you stay here. I will go get it."

"Keep an eye on her?" I turn to Ben.

"Of course," he says, and I go out to the food area and get in line for a bottle of water.

Behind me, I hear a throat clear, and turn to find Jenna's father there.

All we do is stand and stare at each other until it's my turn in line. I get the water for her and me. As I turn to leave, Evans speaks.

"Will you come by the ranch later this week?" is all he says.

"Yeah, I'll be there," I say, turning and going back to Jenna.

I send up a silent prayer that this is a good thing and not the final nail in the coffin of my relationship with him.

Getting to the bleachers, I sit, handing her the water just as the bull riding is getting ready to start.

"I ran into your dad in line," I tell her, and her head snaps up to look at me. "He asked me to come by the ranch later this week. That's all he said, nothing more. I agreed. Though I don't like walking in there blind," I tell her.

"Well, it's a good thing he wants to talk, right?" She says with hope in her voice.

"I think," I say, though my gut doesn't exactly agree.

"Well, when you come home, I will make sure a nice hot bath is waiting for you," she says with a mischievous glint in her eye.

"So long as you are in it," I say with a wink, loving the idea.

Once the bull riding starts, the energy of the whole crowd changes. The excitement is building. The crowd is louder, and more people are on their feet. The gate opens, and the first bull comes out, bucking and spinning. You can feel it when he slams back into the ground. The bleachers shake, and that seems to spur the crowd on even louder. This guy lasted the entire eight seconds, making the crowd go wild.

When it's Finn's turn, the energy around us shifts again. Jenna and I are on our feet, as are her parents and Asher and Zach. Jenna's eyes are on Finn in the gate, her hands covering her mouth. We watch until he gives the nod, and the gate opens, and the bull comes out of the gate spinning and bucking. Time seems to drag on, and those eight seconds feel more like eight minutes as he holds on, swaying back and forth.

The longer he is on the bull, the louder the crowd cheers. It isn't until the rescue crew comes and helps him safely off the back of the bull that Jenna starts yelling. When I take a quick glance at her brothers and her parents, that's when they start cheering, too.

The rest of the riders are a blur, but Finn manages to take home third place and a $10,000 prize for the day.

We head back, where his truck is to meet up with him, and Jenna is there giving him the biggest hug before anyone else. I don't miss a few of the other riders who have their eyes on her the moment she steps away from Finn. Quickly, I pull her back to my side.

"You did great!" she gushes.

"Thanks, the energy out there was really good," Finn says, but his eyes are on the blond that just walked by and winked at him.

"Well, here come Mom and Dad. I'll let you have your time with them. See you at dinner next week." Then we leave him and go back to my truck.

The entire way home, she is enthusing about Finn and how well he did. But all I can think of are all the possible reasons her dad wants to meet with me this week, and not any of them are good.

Chapter 26
JENNA

Since Josh let me sleep in and is already out with the cattle, I am sitting in the dining room having a lazy breakfast. I work later today, so I figured I'd relax and read the new book I got from the library last week. As I'm cleaning up my breakfast dishes, my phone rings. I freeze when I see it's my dad calling. After the last call, I'm not sure I want to pick up, and I almost jump out of my skin when Josh speaks from behind me. I didn't even hear him come in.

"Well, are you going to answer it?" he says.

"It's my dad," I say, staring at it like it's a snake.

"Answer it. I'm right there," he says, removing one of his work gloves and taking my hand in his.

"Hello?" I ask hesitantly, answering the phone.

"Jenna," Dad says. It's not a question, just a statement, and his voice is soft like it used to be when we would talk on the phone.

"Dad," I say, not sure where this conversation is going.

"I'd like for you to stop by and have a chat. The sooner, the better."

I look over at Josh, who just nods.

"Well, I have to work this afternoon, but I could get ready and come that way in a little while."

"That would be wonderful. I'll have your mom make you some lunch," he says, sounding happy.

We hang up, and I stare at my phone.

"That is not the same man from last week."

"Maybe your brother or, hell, anyone else finally got through to him," Josh says, pulling me in for a hug.

"I hope so because if I go over there and he goes off on me, it will be the last time I accept any communication from him. I can't keep going with this anxiety surrounding him."

"I completely get it. Whatever you want to do, I support you one-hundred percent, sweetheart. And sorry I scared you there. I was just coming in to get that replacement part for the tank that came in yesterday."

"Well, I guess I should go get ready for work, and I can go in early and talk with Austin a bit."

"That's a good idea. You know you can invite her or any of your friends over at any time, right? This is your house, too," he reminds me.

Even though he keeps telling me, I still feel like a guest. Maybe it's because I haven't put my touch on the place, or maybe it's because everything with my parents is up in the air. All my stuff is here. It only took Josh's truck and my car to haul the rest of the stuff from my parents to here. It's mostly still in boxes in the spare bedroom. Or maybe I just need to unpack them.

"I was going to see how you felt about doing a girls' night. I really want to have one here, like they do in Rock Springs. Then you and the guys could hang out too?"

"I like it. You girls can have the house, and we will take the back patio. Set it up and let me know when." After grabbing the box off the coffee table, he gives me an all too short kiss before heading back out the door.

I go upstairs, get ready, grab my book, and put it in my purse. If I have extra time, I can sit in the back room at the diner and at least get started on it.

The whole way to my parents' house, my stomach is upset and nerves are jumpy. Trying not to focus on the talk ahead, I crank up my music and focus on it. Though it only helps until I round the corner and see my parents' house. Thankfully, Asher's truck is in the driveway, so he will be there, and I won't be alone. Turning down the music, I pull into the driveway and gather my purse.

But I don't make it even to the porch before the door opens and Asher greets me.

"I'm glad you came," he says, smiling and pulling me in for a hug.

I'm hoping his smile means good things as I follow him to the back of the house to the family room where Mom and Dad are sitting on the couch. They greet me with smiles. So much different than the last time I was here.

I sit on the love seat across from them, and Asher sits in the recliner next to me.

"Thank you for coming. I know things have been rocky, and I wouldn't have blamed you for not even picking up the phone," Dad says.

"I almost didn't. If Josh wasn't there encouraging me to, I probably wouldn't have," I tell him honestly, and he nods.

"Listen, I watched you guys at the rodeo the other day, really watched you. He takes care of you, and the way he looks at you is the way any father would want the man his daughter loves to look at her. I spent many nights wide awake going over everything from the time I met Josh to now. I know him, and while this will take some getting used to, I think I did act a bit harshly. All I thought about is the bad side of it, and I see now that isn't the case here," he says.

"We wanted to talk to you before we talk to Josh. He is coming over later today," Mom says.

"It goes without saying that we really appreciate what he's done for the boys, too, helping them get that ranch," Dad says.

"We just now signed intention paperwork and are moving forward with the bank," Asher says.

"Really? Congrats on that! That's wonderful!" I say to him.

"Yeah, Willy is packing up and invited us to come stay in the bunkhouse so he can teach us everything. Zach has already put in notice at work, and Finn is on board. I just need to get permission from Willy to tell Mrs. Granger what is going on. He still doesn't want it getting out just yet," Asher continues.

"Ahh, she is the biggest gossip in town. I wouldn't even put in your notice if I were you. I'd just tell her you are moving in with your brothers to save money and then work with Willy at night," I tell him.

"See, I told you that, too," Mom says.

"You're right. You know better than anyone who would spill the beans in town. That damn diner is gossip central. It's probably the whole reason you stay there," Asher chuckles.

"Partly, though, it was more of a reason to get out of the house, too," I say.

There is a pause in the conversation, and I look back at my dad.

"We'd like you and Josh to come back to Sunday dinner. Even though it will take some getting used to, and things might be weird, we are asking for the chance to fix this," Dad says.

"We'd also like for you to come home," Mom says.

I don't answer right away. I'm worried my response will shatter the fragile bridge we are building, but I want to be honest with them, too.

"I think Sunday dinners are a good start, but I won't be moving back home. Josh asked me to move in with him, and I have. It's a step we chose to take in our relationship that was outside of all of this. So, I will be staying there," I say.

There is tension in the air, and my dad's jaw is clenched.

"Does this mean we don't get our Thursday night dinners anymore? Because you are a damn good cook, and if I'm moving in with Zach and Finn, the frozen meals will be all I'm eating," Asher pouts.

I just laugh, "I like our Thursday dinners and would love to keep them up. Whenever you feel comfortable, Mom and Dad, we'd love for you to join us." I extend the invitation, but I have a feeling it won't be accepted for quite a while. Sunday dinners will be hard enough to get through.

"Will you stay for lunch?" Mom asks. I made sandwiches, and we'd love to hear what is new with you."

Looking at my phone, I check the time. I have a couple of hours before I have to go to work.

"Sure, I can stay and have lunch with you."

During lunch, we talk and catch up. It was enjoyable, and they were respectful any time I mentioned Josh.

"Well, it's been nice, but I need to go to work," I say after we've eaten and cleaned up.

Mom and Dad both give me an awkward hug and Asher walks me out to my car.

"I don't know what changed their mind or what you did, but I'm grateful."

"It really was seeing you two at the rodeo. Dad said he's never seen you so happy, and Josh was taking good care of you. Maybe what really swayed Dad was how Josh would look at you like you were the only person there."

Nodding, I let that sit in. Basically, the reality of Josh and I together didn't match up with what was in my dad's head, and he had to come to terms with that.

"Will you be here when Josh talks to Dad?" I ask, wanting Josh to have a friendly face around.

"As much as I can be. But I think that will be more of a man-to-man talk without Mom and me there," he says, hugging me and helping me into the car.

I get to work almost an hour early and find Austin in her office answering emails.

Popping my head into her office, I ask her, "Hey, do you have a minute? I just talked to my parents and also have something to talk to you about."

"Of course. Sit down and close the door." She gives me her full attention.

I give her the rundown of what just happened at lunch with my parents.

"That's a good thing, right?" she asks hopefully.

"I think so. I guess it depends on how it goes with Josh later. Though I'm hoping he stops in to let me know about the meeting, because I don't know if I can wait until I get home later."

"Well, I'm so excited for you!" Austin says and jumps up to hug me.

"Well, not so fast. I have one more thing to talk to you about, and you might not like it as much," I tell her, and we both sit back down.

"What's that?"

"I am putting in my two-week notice," I say and wait for her reaction.

She sits there quietly for a moment before she speaks. "I hate to see you go, but to be honest, I'm shocked you stayed this long. Every time you ask to talk to me, I always braced myself. One of the other girls has been asking for more hours, so I will give your shifts to her."

Well, that was a lot easier than I thought. Before starting my shift, I had time to read a little bit and enjoy my book after all the drama. Before I can tell Josh myself, I don't want to let everyone know I'm quitting. So, I figure I'll tell everyone on my next shift.

Just before the dinner rush hits, Dash and Sky walk in and I give them both a hug.

"Perfect timing. I had a meeting with Dad today," I tell them, and Sky's squeals draw everyone's attention.

Anxious to hear my news, they walk with me to the counter. While I fill her in, I make some drinks for the table I just sat. After delivering the drinks, I walk back over to them.

"This is good. And he's talking to Josh today. Oh, I'm so happy for you!" Sky says. "Now, I need some nacho fries, stat. I've been craving them all day."

Before she can sit down at a booth in my section, I ask, "Isn't it too early to have food cravings?"

"I thought so, too," Dash says, but his face lights up as he looks at Sky. I don't think it bothers him one bit.

"Josh and I were talking. I want to have a girls' night like they do in Rock Springs. Josh said the guys could gather on the porch at his... our place. You in?" I ask.

"Of course! Who else are you going to invite?" Sky asks.

"I was thinking Natalie and Jessie, Candy and her husband North, and Austin. Who else should we invite?"

"Maybe Parker? I bet she could use a few friends right now," Sky says.

I agree with her assessment. Everything is coming together. I just hope that Josh's talk with my dad goes smoothly.

Chapter 27
Josh

As I pull into Evan's driveway, I check my phone again. Nothing from Jenna. I was hoping to hear how her talk went, but I guess she has to rush right into work. If it went bad, I know she would have called, so I'm hoping it was all good.

Asher's truck is here, so I'm thankful for a buffer in case this goes wrong like the last time I was here to talk to him. I walk up to the porch and knock on the door.

Evan answers, and we stare at each other for a moment before he steps back and invites me in with a motion of his hand.

"Why don't we head to my office to chat?" he says.

I follow him to the east side of the house where his office sits because he is always up early and likes to watch the sunrise. So when he built the house, he made sure his office was on this side. The master is on the west side because his wife likes to sleep in when possible.

Entering his office, nothing has changed. I take a seat in one of the leather chairs across from his desk, and he sits behind his desk. It's a power move, for sure.

He doesn't say anything at first, so I break the silence.

"Why am I here, Evan?" I ask.

"Jenna didn't talk to you?" he says, surprised.

It makes me wonder what their talk was about.

"No, she must have gone right into work, or I was out of cell service. Did everything go okay?" I ask, suddenly worried.

"I would like to think so. I'm just shocked you haven't talked to her. Well, I'll get started. When I was watching you two at the rodeo, I saw the situation through different eyes. You took care of her and put her needs first. As a father, that is all I ever wanted was for a guy to treat her like a princess."

"She isn't a princess," I say, but he interrupts me.

"No, I know, but I...."

"No, you misunderstand me," I say. "She isn't a princess. She is my queen. My everything, and she will always come first."

We sit there as he digests what I just said and the meaning behind it.

"We talked with Jenna and said we'd like you two to start joining us for Sunday dinner again. It will take some time to get used to the two of you together, so I'm asking for a little grace as we move forward."

"That is up to her. If she wants to come, I will come with her." I say, and he nods.

"I stand by throwing that punch, and when you have a little girl, you will understand," he says.

"I don't have to have a little girl to understand. Though I would have been more shocked if you hadn't punched me."

That earns a smile from him.

"Thank you for helping the boys with the ranch. They are moving forward and are very excited. "

"I'm happy to help. Those boys are family." I tell him, and he nods.

We sit in silence for a few minutes, and again, I am the one to break it.

"You get that damn car up and going yet?"

"That thing is more stubborn than Jenna is. Could use an extra pair of hands on it this weekend," he says.

And just like that, I know we will be okay. But there is one more thing I need to handle first.

"I'm more than happy to help. But Evan?" I say and wait until he is looking at me.

"I'd like your blessing to ask Jenna to marry me. Either way, I plan to ask her. But it would mean more to have your blessing to do so." I say, waiting.

I can tell he isn't happy because he's glaring at me.

"You couldn't wait until we got used to the idea of you two together first?" he says, clearly annoyed.

"When you knew Janet was it for you, did you want to wait?" I ask.

Slamming his hand down on his desk, he stands and walks over to the window. He stands there quietly, looking out at the part of the lake he can see. I can't even guess what is going through his head.

"You are the best man I know, Josh. Hardworking and loyal. Everything I have always wanted for her, yet it's still hard for me to be okay with you two together."

My heart sinks that he won't give his blessing, but I plan to make Jenna my wife anyway, and I'm okay with that. He will grow to be all right with us. Then he abruptly turns to face me.

"I will give you my blessing, but just know if you hurt her, the punch I gave you will seem like a feather kiss compared to the punishment you will get," he declares.

He gave me his blessing! I can't believe my ears. While I know we still have a long road ahead of us, at least Jenna will be at my side. That is all that matters.

• • • • • • • • •

Jenna

I was really hoping Josh would come into the diner after his talk with my dad, but I haven't heard a word. So, I wrapped up my shift a bit early and texted him.

On my way home.

See you when you get here.

I don't even know what to make of that. I hope it went well, and he's just busy. That would be the best-case scenario. In the worst case, it didn't go well, and I'm not going to like the talk that is ahead of us tonight. If needed, I'm ready to fight for us. Now that I have my parents back, I'm not giving up.

Once I arrive home, before I even get the door closed, I go inside, calling out his name. Though, I'm surprised he hasn't answered me. Taking off my shoes, I hang up my purse and go to the kitchen to look for him. That's when I see the line of red rose petals leading to a path at the back of the house. I follow them to the back door, where there is a piece of paper taped to it, and in Josh's handwriting is a note.

Jenna,

Get changed into one of those cute dresses you like to wear and meet me in the barn.

Josh

Rushing upstairs, I grab one of the dresses I wore a few weeks ago that he liked so much. After slipping the dress on, I put on my cowboy boots and go to the barn. I don't know what I'm looking for, but when I get there, I find Dolly groomed and with bows in her hair. There is an envelope attached to one of the bows with my name on it. I remove it and read it.

Jenna,
We have made a good team, but I think it's time to add one.
Dolly

It's signed Dolly, but it's in Josh's handwriting and I have no idea what he means by one more. Another horse? I glance at the stalls nearby, and they are empty. When I turn around, I found Josh behind me, down on one knee with a ring box in his hand. It's all I can do to stand because my knees are about to give out.

"I know things with us haven't been easy, and I can't promise they ever will be. But I can promise to love you until my last breath, to show you how much I love you every day, and to help you follow your dreams. I can also promise you I will always take care of you and support you. I can promise I will always be by your side and love you unconditionally. Marry me and be my wife. Start a family with me and be at my side."

By the time he stops, the tears are pouring uncontrollably down my face.

"Yes. It's always been yes." I say, falling into his arms.

He holds me for a few minutes before he puts the ring on my finger.

"I take it the talk with my dad went good?" I laugh, trying to wrap my head around it all.

"It did. He even gave me his blessing to marry you." He says it with a huge smile lighting up his eyes.

"Really? He did?" I say, shocked.

"Yep, he did, Josh says grinning big. "Sunday dinners are officially reinstated. They will get used to us. Hopefully, by the time he is walking you down the aisle."

"Oh my god, I have to call Sky and Sarah. We have so much planning to do!"

"Slow down, sweetheart. The only plan you have to do tonight is what positions I'm going to have you in because I don't plan to let you out of bed for at least twenty-four hours."

"I think I can get used to that," I smile.

Epilogue
Asher

W e closed on the ranch today, and the three of us stand here still in shock. Willy moved out yesterday, and we stayed at our parents' house last night, not wanting to be here alone until it was ours. So tonight will be our first night sleeping in the main house as ranch owners.

Mom and Dad are here, and so are Jenna and Josh. Surrounded by family at one of the biggest times in our lives, still doesn't make it feel real.

"We are ranch owners," I say out loud.

"We own Silver Cattle Ranch," Finn says.

"Best of all, Finn's most recent rodeo earning is buying your first herd of cattle," Josh says with a laugh.

We found a ranch just west of here that was being foreclosed on and selling the cattle at a reasonable price.

"It still doesn't seem real," I say as we stand in the front yard of the old farmhouse and stare at it. It's a four bedroom and is plenty big for us to live in while we get started and still have office space.

Zach and Finn decided that I'll take this house because they want to build something newer and have already picked out the plot of land for their homes on the far corners of the ranch.

"Well, let's head inside so Jenna and I can figure out how to decorate it for you boys," Mom says.

"We also need to see what furniture you are going to need. I know Willy said he's left some," Dad says.

When we go inside, the place looks empty compared to the last time we were here.

"Wow, Willy left this place in great condition," Dad says.

The wood floors have all been recently polished, and he left a couch and the dining room table.

"These are brand new appliances," Josh says.

When I walk into the kitchen, I see it's true. He replaced the appliances with brand-new ones.

"Same with the washer and drier. They are brand new, too," Mom says, coming out of the mudroom where the washer and dryer are.

"I can't believe he did that," I say.

"Just wanted to make sure you had the best possible start," Willy says from the open front door.

I've prided myself on keeping my emotions close to my chest ever since the girl I dated in high school broke my heart, but this man right here is making my eyes tear up. I walk over and pull the old man into a hug.

"Hey, now, none of that. I also left you three new beds in the bedrooms. They have to be put together, but at least you will have somewhere to sleep tonight."

"Thank you for this," I say, knowing there really are no words that can express what this means to us.

"Well, knowing this ranch went to someone who wants it as much as I did is all the thanks I need. Just like my granddaddy said to me. If at any point you go to sell it, make sure it goes to someone who wants to run the ranch, not the land," Willy says.

"We will, but I don't see us selling anytime soon."

"Good. Now excuse me, I need to get on the road. I have a hot date waiting for me." Willy turns and walks through the door yelling, "Arizona, here I come!" Then gets in his car and drives away.

I watch Willy go. Even once his car is out of sight, I continue standing on the front porch, enjoying the view. I can hardly believe that is my view from my front porch. Then a truck I know very well with a trailer on it starts down the driveway. When it parks, I walk over, "Mrs. Granger, what are you doing here?" I ask.

It was hard putting in my notice with her. She and her husband have talked to me so much and taken me under their wing. I dreaded that conversation, but they were overjoyed when I told them we finally got a place and which one it was. They insisted we let them help any way they could, and of course, we'd take them up on it.

"Well, you didn't think you'd sneak away and never see us again, did you, boy?" She says with her customary sass.

"No ma'am," I say with a smile.

"Good. Now Finn, get over here!" She calls my brother, who is on the front porch.

"On the passenger side, there are enough meals to feed you for a month. Put them in the freezer, and the directions are on top," she says.

"You didn't have to do that, but thank you," I say.

"That I did have to do. You boys were planning on frozen meals. Don't even lie to me. Now this," she says, starting toward the trailer. "This I didn't have to do, but after all the years of work you did, and how often you went above and beyond, it's well deserved."

Zach, Josh, and my dad have joined us at the back of the trailer, and through the slats, another pair of eyes I know all too well looks at us.

"Rocky?" I ask, shocked to see one of their best bulls in the trailer.

"Yep, it was time for us to bring in a new bull anyway, and heifers are cheap, but a good bull will be hard to come by. This should keep you in the black for at least a few years. Now, where do you want him?"

I turn to look at Josh with my eyes wide, and he chuckles.

"Put him in the small field by the barn for now," Josh says.

After I agree, Zach helps her with as I stand there still in shock.

When they head to the barn, the sound of tires crunching gravel fills the air from behind me. I turn and find a little four-door car pull into the driveway. No one I know would try to drive these roads with a car like that. I wait to see who it belongs to, and before long, a woman with long, straight black hair, steps out of the car and turns to me. Something in the air shifts.

"You must be Asher," she says, removing her sunglasses and walking toward me with a folder in her hand.

"Should I be worried you know my name, but I don't know yours?" I ask.

"It's a small town. People talk," she shrugs. Her deep brown eyes take me in. "I'm Kassi."

The name doesn't ring a bell, but I don't know everyone in town either.

"Well, it's nice to meet you. What can I do for you?"

"It's what I can do for you," she says.

Suddenly I have pictures of her laid out on my bed doing plenty of stuff for me, but I doubt that is what she means.

She hands me the folder, and I glance at it.

Lunar Land Developing.

"That offer is more than generous and good for one year from today."

"We just bought this place. Why would we sell?" I say, instantly irritated.

"The ranch may not be all it's cracked up to be. My boss wants you to know we are serious about the land." She turns and goes back to her car. "Take a look. It's a good offer." She says this more softly as she gets in the car.

As she drives off, I realize I'm in so much trouble. That girl works with the enemy.

And she's going to be mine.

• • • ● • ● • • • •

Want more Jenna and Josh? **Grab the Bonus Epilogue now!**

Grab Asher's story next in **The Cowboy and His Enemy!**

Get Mac and Sarah's story in **The Cowboy and His Secret!**

More Books by Kaci M. Rose

The Cowboy and His Secret – Mac and Sarah
Rock Springs Weddings Novella

Cowboys of Rock Springs

The Cowboy and His Mistletoe Kiss – Lilly and Mike
The Cowboy and His Valentine – Maggie and Nick
The Cowboy and His Vegas Wedding – Royce and Anna
The Cowboy and His Angel – Abby and Greg
The Cowboy and His Christmas Rockstar – Savannah and
Ford
The Cowboy and His Billionaire – Brice and Kayla
The Cowboy and His Sleeping Beauty – Miles and Rose

Connect with Kaci M. Rose

Kaci M. Rose writes steamy small town cowboys. She also writes under Kaci Rose and there she writes wounded military heroes, giant mountain men, sexy rock stars, and even more there. Connect with her below!

Website

Kaci M Rose's Book Store

Facebook

Kaci Rose Reader's Facebook Group

Goodreads

Book Bub

Join Kaci M. Rose's VIP List (Newsletter)

About Kaci M Rose

Kaci M Rose writes cowboy, hot, and steamy cowboys set in all towns anywhere you can find a cowboy.

She enjoys horseback riding and attending rodeos, always looking for inspiration.

Kaci grew on a small farm/ranch in Florida where they raised cattle and an orange grove. She learned to ride a four-wheeler instead of a bike (and to this day, still can't ride a bike) and was driving a tractor before she could drive a car.

Kaci prefers the country to the city to this day and lives in the mountains of East Tennessee with cows and horses as her neighbors.

Kaci M Rose is the Cowboy Romance alter ego of Author Kaci

Rose.

See all of Kaci Rose's Books here.

Please Leave a Review!

I love to hear from my readers! Please **head over to your favorite store and leave a review** of what you thought of this book! Reviews also appreciated on BookBub and Goodreads!

Made in United States
Troutdale, OR
03/17/2024